The L
of
Cregheligan

This paperback first edition published in 2025 by Karl R. Harter
publishing@karlrharter.net

British Library Cataloguing-in-Publication Data
A catalogue record of this book is available on request from the British Library

ISBN 978-1-0369-1278-9

Set in Source Serif Pro, an open-source serif typeface designed by Frank Grießhammer and released by Adobe Systems. Source Serif Pro is licensed under the SIL Open Font License, Version 1.1, and is freely available for commercial and non-commercial use.

Printed and bound in Great Britain by
CPI Group (UK) Ltd, Croydon, CR0 4YY

Thank you

To JJ, for believing in me, and enabling me to complete this book.

To Christian, for encouraging me to continue, and for putting me in touch with Rosie, without whom I would not have this wonderful artwork.

To Michael, for the motivation to carry on.

Chapter 1
First Day of Summer

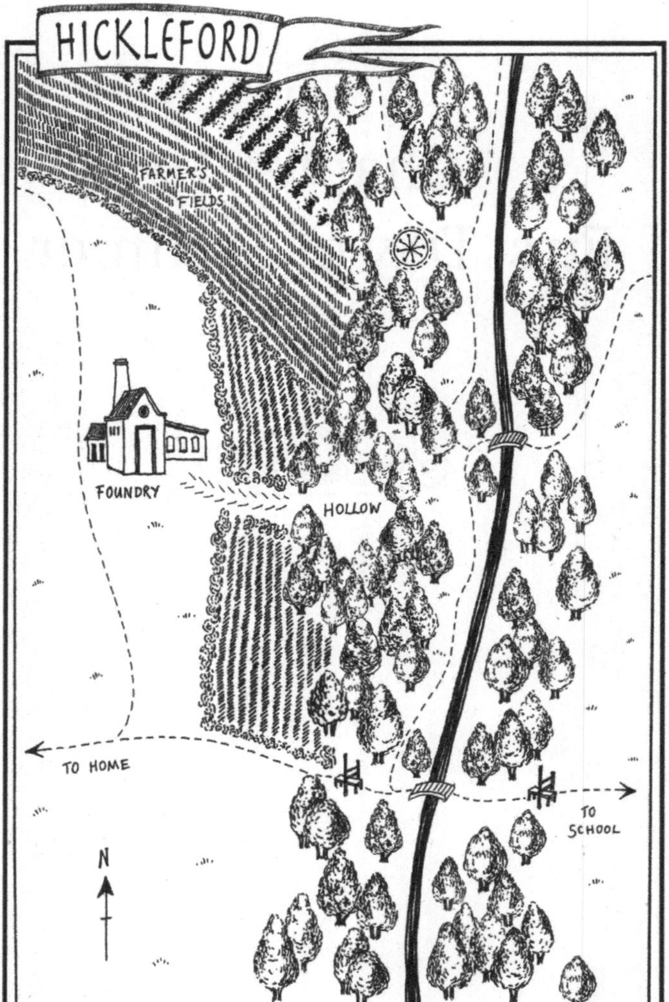
HICKLEFORD
FARMER'S FIELDS
FOUNDRY
HOLLOW
TO HOME
TO SCHOOL
N

A late afternoon summer sunshine edged its rays through tall leafy trees, standing either side of the lane like soldiers on parade. Hazy, dry warmth filled the air, providing a gentle breeze for butterflies to dither around in. The atmosphere filled with innumerable measure of insect activity, most too faint for the eye to see while passing. The height of summer fell upon the nation, and with it, came freedom.

School was over, it was the start of summer holidays, the start of what would seem like a lifetime to the herds of children that began to pour from the schoolyard. Younger ones at first, delicately whisked away by parents. Then the bells rang out, and like a flurry of ants from a hill they spilled out onto the lane. Marauding, miniature warriors filled the battlefield known as Chapel Lane, heading not for war, but home to parents, pets and playthings alike. School was conquered at last, well, at least for this year.

'Race you to the farm gate.' shouted Tom, pelting down the lane, Damien laughed and chased after, followed by a scattering of others.

Tom reached the gate, placing both hands on the top bar he vaulted into the air landing gracefully on the dusty track beyond. Damien copied and the pair ran on, clouds of dust trailing behind as they laughed at their life of freedom ahead.

Both boys were 14 years of age, Tom slightly older, a fact he occasionally reminded Damien of if ever there happened to be a disagreement between the two. Not that Damien took any notice, he generally displayed the finger in gross disrespect for his elder, at which point a wrestle would ensue. Ultimately one would have the other in an arm lock or similar method of restraint, and the disagreement was resolved. The pair had been friends from junior school and spent most of their spare time together. When not exploring uncharted forests at the bottom of their housing estate, they would often be found engaged in combat, over at Tom's house on his Play Station.

The warm summer breeze gently swayed the wheat fields surrounding the track along which they ran. Approaching the wooded valley, two pigeons lifted into the air, wings clapping at the sight of these invaders. Curling above the trees the birds made their escape to the far side of the wood. The occasional croaking of a distant pheasant added to the activity, enriching the atmosphere of this special place. By now the heat had blunted the boys' competitive edge, panting up to the stile and into the wood. Clambering over, they entered another world, a world of mystery and darkness. A world of moss-covered roots and deep earthy aromas, snatching at the lungs with the scent of wild garlic and pungent vegetation.

A thin, well-trodden path led off down the slope. The forest, set in a steep valley, acted like a border between home and school. A stream flowed south through the middle, separating the good of home-life and evil of school. It was truly a beautiful place, a place where ancient trees heaved skyward. Broad reaching emerald canopies cast a green glow over everything beneath. In midday sunlight this place was paradise, at dusk, it filled with unseen demons lurking behind tree trunks, and goblins hunched deep within crevices. Creatures awaiting the unwary, or at least it seemed. Staggering down the track and into the wooded valley, Tom and Damien excitedly planned their future explorations.

'So, we meet at six o'clock tonight after Tea, I'll come to your house and we can head to for the foundry.' declared Tom.

'Cool, and if we fail this time, I'm taking up golf or

something.'

'Golf!' blurted Tom 'Dad says golf just spoils a good walk.'

A confused expression washed over Damien's face, gradually turning into a broad smile. 'Yeah, your dad's right.'

The foundry, was an old Iron foundry, little more than a fenced off yard now, but with some machinery and a chimney still in place. The new starting point for this week's exploration. Their mission was to find a way into the patch of woodland known as the hollow, an area inaccessible from the forest itself. A wheat field, regularly patrolled by an angry farmer and his psychopathic dog proved impossible to avoid. The hollow had already claimed one trouser leg and inflicted several barbed wire cuts, so this time called for a more careful approach. The hollow was a place of mystery, a place for sinister creatures to hide and a place for treasure to be found. It was a place that no one had ever entered, or at least ever returned from. In reality, it was just a natural dip in the ground. A hollow in the middle of a field, about half the size of a football pitch. It was filled with trees and brambles, nettles and bracken. The hollow was part of the wooded valley, yet the two were separated by fields. These fields became the obstacle which prevented the boys from exploring this perceived paradise.

Upon reaching the far side of the wooded valley, the boys made their way through a gate that led out of the woods and onto a track. The track sliced its way through grazing fields on either side. In the distance, set on a rise of land, lay the housing estate where the two boys lived. Beyond the estate was the town, a place neither of them had much interest in. The real enjoyment was exploration, and they had perfect surroundings for it.

'Right then, so six o'clock at my house?' Said Damien.

'Cool, and bring your dad's torch just in case.' Replied Tom.

Damien shuddered and acknowledged, remembering the time they found themselves at the north end of the wood without a torch as the sun went down. A terrifying experience that neither of them would wish to repeat, requiring nerves of steel and fast legs to escape the unseen which followed them. Reaching the end of the path the pace had slowed to little more than a trudge. Each, in turn, stepped over another stile, crossed a stretch of open ground and climbed the slope onto the end of a cul-de-sac. It was here they went their separate ways.

The estate was dull compared to the intensity of colours in the forest. Semi-detached houses and bungalows lined the roads. A land of little more than red-tiled rooftops, white double glazing and well-trimmed lawns. All of which made for a bland impression in comparison to the forest. Tom and Damien loved the outdoors, in summer they would spend days exploring. Knee deep in wellies paddling through the stream, lifting up boulders, searching for treasure, fishing for guppies or simply constructing dens. Sometimes, if they were really lucky, they would get permission to camp out overnight in each other's back garden. They hadn't yet been granted permission to go beyond the garden, but this didn't matter to them. In the early hours of the morning simply being outdoors created its own unique environment. Silvered, misty dew on grass, strange animal noises that could only be heard before dawn. The crisp, damp coldness of early-morning, biting at uncovered faces peeping out of sleeping bags. All these experiences were absorbed while camping, it was addictive. At heart, they were explorers, conquerors in search of new lands, and this passion for exploration was greater than anything else to them.

Hinckleford wasn't a particularly large town, but the place was a friendly one. Most people who lived there were born there and generally spent their lives there too. Tom's father was a joiner and worked for a small firm on the far side of town, while Damien's father was a plumber. The boy's fathers met every Friday night at the local pub, then on Saturday all four parents would meet up at the social club in town.

Many of their friend's parents did the same, the kids got away with nothing. Every knock and run, every prank and every brawl went noticed. Each misdemeanour reported at the weekly social club gathering, and each adequately awarded punishment, the severity of which was dependant on the degree of mischief itself. This was probably the reason the boys headed for the woods, it was their last hope of undisturbed freedom!

Chapter 2
The Hollow

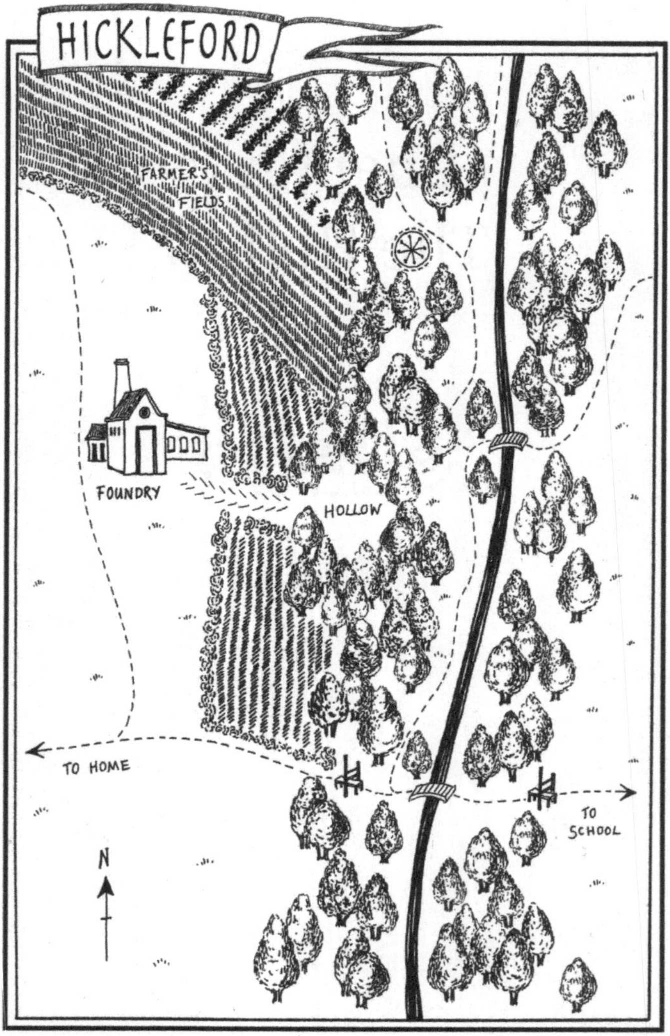
HICKLEFORD
FARMER'S FIELDS
FOUNDRY
HOLLOW
TO HOME
TO SCHOOL
N

Six O'clock came and with it a knock at Damien's front door.

'See you later Mum, I'm off out to the woods with Tom.' shouted Damien, swinging a half empty rucksack over his shoulder.

'Alright, but I want you back in this house by nine O'clock tonight, do you hear?'

He did, but was too far out of the house to reply, the mission was underway.

Dressed more like underpaid mercenaries than explorers, the pair set off through the estate then North along a country lane. Winding their way through fields and farmyards they reached a patch of disused industrial ground, at the far end stood the foundry.

'So, if we get spotted by the farmer again, we head for the woods and split up like last time.' Ever the organiser, Tom directed the escape and evasion plan should the mission fail at stage one. They knew that by splitting up only one of them was likely to get caught. Loyalty was steadfast and neither one of them would ever break, even under the harshest of punishment, or at least until their parents found out.

The foundry stood silent, foreboding, fenced off like an old wooden palisade. Loose timber fencing surrounding a tall watchtower-like chimney. They had been here before, but never tried to venture inside, once again another giant leap for boy-kind.

'There, to the right of the gate, there's a gap in the bottom of the fence.' Tom pointed and led the way. Checking around for onlookers, just like in the gangster movies right before the hit, he pushed through. Damien followed on.

Beyond the fence loomed grey skeletons of industry. Tom paused motionless, ash and dust covered the floor like radioactive fallout. Rusting iron ingots piled high against the far brick wall of the factory. A miniature rail track ran down from a ramp attached to the chimney, disappearing off into a shed at the far end of the yard. Stepping back in time, like a dream come true, a gold mine from a black and white movie, everything grey and drab looking.

'Wow this is awesome!' Damien gasped 'It's completely preserved, we should make a base here.'

Tom cautiously checked for signs of inhabitants 'Do you think anyone comes here?' conscious of the fact they had broken in.

'I doubt it, nothing has been touched since they closed it down.' Damien's focus was on the adventure, not the risk. 'They probably don't even use this kind of foundry anymore; it's like a film set.'

The pair forgot their mission and started to explore the far shed, a pile of coke cinders, iron ingots and a broken cart. Gradually it all started to take shape.

'Look, they used the cart to wheel ore up the ramp and into the furnace, and below is the fire door for raking out the ash.' Tom continued to intricately patch together evidence, delivering his opinion of how the place ran. Whether this was accurate neither could be sure, but it sounded about right. Within several minutes a whole working practice had been developed and delivered to a half listening Damien, who was rapidly constructing his own opinions on the site.

'Ok, I think we should stop now and continue with the original plan' suggested Tom 'this place needs some real work, we might even be able to get this going again.' Scrutinising the pulley and cart system.

'Let's find a way to the hollow from here.' Tom knew that if they didn't break this off now, there was a risk of forgetting the reason they were here.

Leaving the shed they walked slowly through the yard, Tom scrutinised the distant fence for a clue. Then there it was, to the rear of one of the large sheds, a gap in the fence, no more than couple of hands wide. Tom ran over and peered through, beyond the crumbling fence post there was a deep drainage ditch which ran down through the field.

'This is it!' said Tom, 'This is the way in, you can't see this ditch from the farm or the track, and that's why we haven't noticed it before.' Tom felt a lightness in his breath as his pulse began to flutter with excitement. He pushed, forcing himself through the gap, taking splinters of fence along with him. Damien followed, scrambling down into the dry ditch. The ditch was about two meters wide and one and a half deep, heads low they scurried along like a pair of rats. They needn't have bothered, the ditch provided ample cover from onlookers. Sunken out of sight in a natural dip in the ground.

The sky was starting to fade into orange, afternoon turned to evening and a tangerine glow cast across the fields, cooling the air to a more comfortable level. Tom approached the bramble hedge surrounding the hollow. Fine splinters of fence wood still clung to his jacket, crouching wide eyed he looked for a way in. Beyond the bramble barricade, broad oak trees stood like giants guarding a sacred space. Tom scrambled out of the ditch and brushed his way through the thicket. Damian followed on, holding back muffled yelps as brambles snagged and pulled. Once inside, the smell of bracken and undergrowth overpowered their senses, this was indeed a mystical place. The trees were ancient here, thick trunks towering up from soft ground, cushioned by a blanket of untouched bracken. A thick fog of vegetation offered up ample cover, and a soft green carpet to welcome the newcomers.

Tom stood for a moment, motionless and stinging from a myriad of bramble scratches. His lungs filled with pachouli scented surroundings and a cool, crisp dampness.

'This place is amazing.' Said Tom, plucking a thorn from the back of his left hand. Damien acknowledged, his face red with excitement as he nodded and scanned around. They edged their way down the slope to the centre and into a clearing at the bottom. The ground was damp, sloping gently down to a small weed-covered pond. Moss hugged the lower tree trunks, as ivy stretched its way upward, clinging to the bark in search of light.

'Ok, I'm starving, let's eat.' Tom, slumping down onto a fallen tree, exhausted from the rush of adrenalin, began to fumble through his pack for provisions. Side by side they sat and broke open their rations. Feeling smug and content with their achievement they celebrated with a sandwich.

'I think we could make a base here too; it doesn't look like anyone else comes here.' Damien began to plan the site. 'We could camp here! A secret camping ground. Over in that area we could build a shelter, this could be the cooking area, and over in that space; wait, what's that?' Damien paused, staring at the ground ahead. Stuffing a half-eaten sandwich into his mouth, he stood up and walked cautiously over to an object protruding from the ground. Carefully brushing away the leaves and dirt he revealed a leather-bound book.

'Hey, look at this,' mumbled Damien through a mouthful of bread 'it's an old book.'

'Bring it over, let's see.'

The book was the size of a postcard and as thick as a matchbox, several old pages delicately stitched into a tattered, brown leather cover. Damien crouched beside Tom and opened it up. The inside cover featured a map spread across two pages with a rough terrain outline marked upon it. On the map there was a circle in the top right corner and a cross in the centre at the bottom. Each of the other pages had inscriptions written on them, ten in total, but none were legible. Although the map was old it appeared to resemble the area that they were in, the cross was in the hollow and the circle appeared to be in the woodland beyond.

'What do you think it's supposed to be?' asked Damien.

Tom took hold of the book, its pages thick as leather, rough and damp to the touch.

'It looks like a book of poems the way it's set out, but I don't recognise the language?'

'I don't think it is a language' added Damien 'if it is, then it's nothing I've seen before.'

The inscriptions were faint, more like scrapings than actual text. They examined the book in more detail while tucking into their sandwiches. Like a pair of forensic scientists, scrutinising and prodding each seam and page, searching for a secret fold or pocket. They found nothing, it appeared to be little more than a tatty old book.

The light was beginning to fade, and with it, an eerie cold silence spread across the hollow. After finishing their snack, they started to look around for other treasures, but it soon became impossible without using a torch, and that might have given away their position.

'I think we should start to head back soon' suggested Damien 'before it gets dark?'

'Yeah, I bet this place is pretty spooky at night, let's come back in the morning and explore the remainder.' Tom added, taking one last kick at a rotten log, revealing nothing but a few wood lice and a centipede, which rippled itself to safety beneath a rotting leaf.

Damien slid the book into his pack, tightened the draw string, and started to walk back up the slope.

Cold, damp air filled the hollow as they reached the top and into what daylight there was left. They broke from cover, this time with Damien in the lead. Smashing through brambles and straight into the ditch, a little easier than the first time. Then began their scurry back to the foundry. Heads low avoiding detection, just as before, well trained, focusing only on survival and evading capture.

'That place is pretty scary; I wouldn't like to stay there after dark.' panted Tom, feeling the sting as he spat and wiped the dried blood stain from the back of his hand.

'We were thinking of camping there a few minutes ago until I found that book.' Laughed Damien, feeling a little more at ease in the open ground. The fence was exactly how they left it, cautiously squeezing through they entered the yard.

'Let's take a closer look at that book again while there's still some light.' Tom paused, brushing off splintered wood and thorns from his jacket and trouser legs.

Damien retrieved the book and handed it to Tom. Turning to the first page he studied the map again, squinting with a look of confusion. 'I thought the cross was in the hollow on the map.'

'It is, and the circle is in the Woods.'

'Well, not anymore.'

'What?'

'The circle is in the same place, but the cross has moved!'

'What! Show me that' Damien took the book from Tom and studied the map 'that's impossible! I'm sure it wasn't there before.' The map picture had changed. Instead of just showing the hollow and forest beyond, the scale of the map had increased. The cross was now situated in a field to the west of the hollow, and other prominent features were displayed on the map, such as the dusty track they walked down to reach the foundry. This was an ancient map of the place they were in, and it appeared to have adjusted according to their location.

Tom looked on in disbelief at what they had found.

'I think we have a change of plan for tomorrow.' A shiver ran down his back as he began to think about what this could mean. 'It's like a Medieval Sat-Nav!' Tom sniggered as he took back the book and studied the map again, it was just an old thick sheet of paper, no different from any other, but the cross had moved.

The pair eased themselves back through the gap beside foundry gate and onto the track, checking and re-checking the map for changes on their way home. Sure enough, each time the book was opened the cross had moved.

'I think we need to keep this a secret, if word of this book gets out, we are likely to lose it.'

'Agreed, it's too good a find to talk about in public.' replied Damien.

Tom's head swirled with thoughts of what this could be, not even the scratches on his arms and legs could distract from the intensity of thoughts he tried to make sense of now. On reaching Damien's house, the pair went inside, quickly kicking off shoes they ran upstairs to his room. Damien took out the book again. The cross had moved even further away from the circle; and the scale of the map had changed again. When turning the page, the texts appeared to have faded even more and where barely visible.

'Do you want to stay over tonight?' Asked Damien nervously.

'Well, I don't fancy taking that thing home on my own.'

They both laughed at the thought of what powers the book might hold, then Damien went downstairs to check it was okay for Tom to stay.

On returning, Damien found Tom staring at the book.

'It almost feels alive, where do you think it came from?'

'I have no idea, but I think we are going to find out tomorrow.' Damien stood by the window and gazed out towards the woods 'The circle has something to do with this, it hasn't moved and always remains on the page wherever you open the book.'

'Tomorrow we should go find it in the forest.' Suggested Tom, hoping Damien would suggest something wiser, safer, but also knowing he wouldn't.

Damien's mum brought them some juice and prepared a sofa bed on the floor of Damien's room.

'Ok, I think it's time for bed now you two.' A little surprised at how obedient they seemed. 'Everything alright? You two look like you've seen a ghost!'

The pair looked at each other and laughed.

'Goodnight mum!'

Chapter 3
Dornachrov

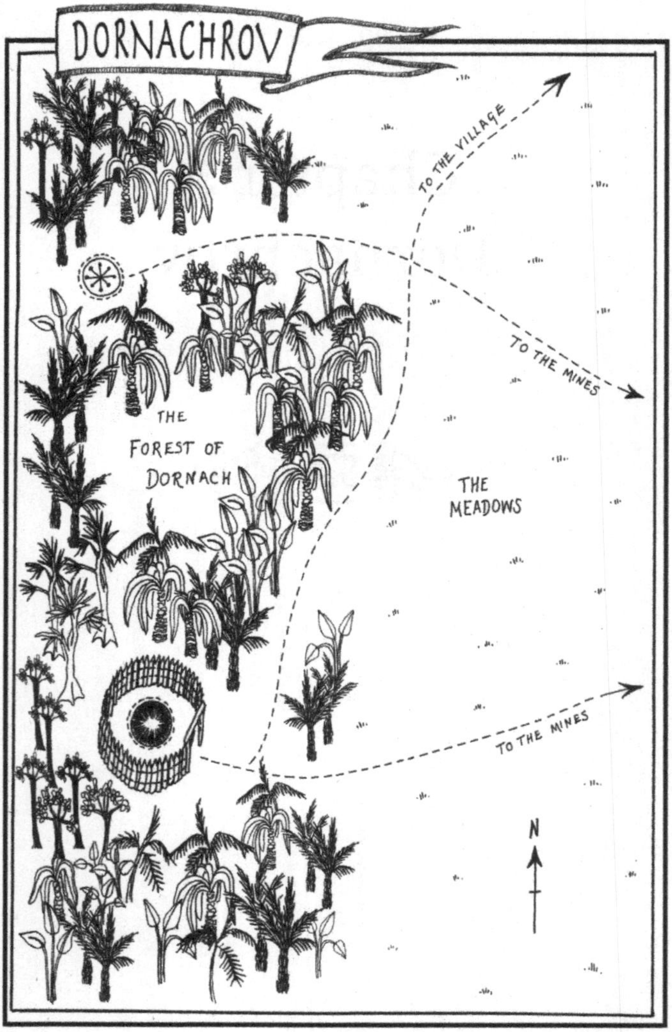
DORNACHROV
TO THE VILLAGE
TO THE MINES
THE FOREST OF DORNACH
THE MEADOWS
TO THE MINES
N

Tom woke around eight o'clock, the sun shining through the window. *It was going to be another warm sunny day and they would need plenty of provisions to get through this one.*

Crouched, he peered out of the window and into the distance. He could just make out the tree tops of the wood, green, summery and still, like a painting by one of those famous artists he could never remember the name of. Damien yawned and pushed back the quilt.

'What time is it?'

'Just after eight, time to get ready I recon.' Replied Tom, now standing at the window, still half in his sleeping bag and holding it tight around his waist, half boy, half caterpillar. Damien sat up, stretched, swung his legs to the floor and made his way to the bathroom, leaving Tom to his thoughts.

Showering reawakened the stings of bramble scars from the previous day. When both had showered, they trudged downstairs to find buttered toast for breakfast, after which, Tom ran home to re-pack his bag. The boys each carried the same kit, torch, matches, penknife, string, notebook, pencil, the list went on. This was a familiar routine for them, they were well accustomed to exploration, every possible item they might require was sought and stowed carefully. Each boy carried the same kit, packed slightly differently, but this time more care was taken. This time felt more real than before. This time they might need every item rather than carry without purpose. Like soldiers fresh out of training, for the first time it felt like they were about to encounter the real thing. What exactly the real thing was, they had no idea, but a find as rich as this book must mean something.

When Tom returned freshly packed, they left the house. It was just after nine o'clock as they set off for the forest, taking the usual track across the field. The day was already starting to warm up, butterflies and other insects dried the morning dew from their wings in the sunlight, the grass was still damp underfoot in some places. The hollow in the field to the North, looked tiny from this point, hardly the place it was last night, and nowhere near as intimidating.

'It's hard to believe we found a way into that place.' Tom muttered to himself gazing toward the treetops.

'I'll take a look at the map and see where we need to be heading.' Damien pulled out the book and opened it up, the cross had moved again, this time it was by the edge of the Wood, the exact spot that they were standing in. 'What do you think we'll find when we get there?'

'I have no idea, but it better be good, I don't do this early on days off.' Tom smiled, at the same time trying to hide his apprehension, he was nervous, but knew he couldn't show it. The pair laughed and continued on, as the daylight worked hard at granting them newfound courage. Tom reached the stile first and climbed over. Entering the underworld of the forest; it was cooler here as they half-skidded and hopped their way down the slope of the valley. When they reached the stream at the bottom Damien checked the map again and pointed north.

Leaving the main track, they branched off North along a lesser used path which ran parallel with the stream. At this time of day, the forest was alive with wildlife, tiny wrens flirted in and around the bank of the stream, unconcerned with the two explorers as the stream frothed and bubbled along its route. The croaky echoing call of a cock pheasant sounded in the distance, encouraging a cackle from several rooks somewhere high above. As the boys moved closer, the anticipation of what was to come grew stronger, the deeply pungent scent of vegetation around them grabbed at each breath as they worked their way along the stream. The scent reminded Tom of the hollow and the bramble scratch on his left hand, it started to itch. The bridge came into view, it was an old wooden construction providing access from one farm to another. Too flimsy for cattle, but just wide enough for two people to cross at once. Beyond the bridge, on the eastern bank of the stream was a small grassy clearing either side of the track. On the western side to the left, the track split and snaked its way up towards the top of the valley.

Damien stopped by the bridge and opened the book again.

'This way.' Taking the lead, he guided them up a gentle slope with the book open.

'It isn't moving!'

'It brought us this far' Tom said with a confused tone 'try closing the book and reopening it.'

'You mean switch it off and on again?' Damian laughed. 'Dad says folk earn a fortune in IT support just for saying that.'

He did as Tom suggested, sure enough, the cross had moved, and it was closer to the circle. A little further up the track Damien re-opened the book. The cross had moved again.

'Right stop here, we need to go left and off the track, there behind those trees!' Tom felt a pang of fear and excitement shift through him as Damien pointed out a partially enclosed ring of trees. Leaving the track, he bounded through the trees towards the area, Tom followed. Reaching the circle he paused just before entering, allowing Tom to catch up. Tom's thoughts took hold. *Am I the only one feeling anxious about this?* A cool trickle of sweat ran down from his neck.

Together they walked through the ring of trees and began to look around, it was about the size of a tennis court. The clearing was surrounded by Yew trees, their roots covered in thick green moss, canopies reaching out to each other above. This place had an ancient feel about it, again the air was cooler here, the ground flat and dry, chilled with a haunting silence. The boys looked at each other, then peered down to the book in Damien's hands. The title on the cover was readable "The Book of Cregheligan." They held the book between them and slowly opened a page; the cross had moved and was in the centre of the circle. Damien's fingers trembled; his mouth dry as he slowly fumbled the next page over. The text was readable, every page had a title and a passage of text beneath it.

Dornachrov
Esbardach
Undacragov
Elmatoch
Pasdron
Relifra
Lowenwrach
Evensithe
Eldegreth
Merwag ed Wroth

The last page simply had the title and nothing below it.

'Should we read one?' asked Tom, but before he had got an answer Damien had already started to recite the text on the first page.

'Elders of the book of Cregheligan,
we seek channel to Dornachrov,
through worlds afar,
part the elements,
part time and space,

through the void of existence grant this journey.'

As the last word was spoken a shade gradually fell upon the area, a cold deathly shade like the end of time itself. The ground started to gently vibrate and all around them fell from focus. The boys stood aghast as their world began to run like a watercolour painting in the rain.

'Monet!' whispered Tom, that was the painter he could never remember 'Claude Monet.'

Colours faded and merged into one another, shades turned to darkness and a strong earthy scented mist filled the atmosphere. A scent of an ancient time and place. A deep echoing sound grew stronger, pounding, reverberating through the bones like a kettle drum. Then, as slowly as it crept in, the mist began to clear, the vibrations ebbed away, the air felt humid on the skin and warm through the lungs. This didn't feel like that summer's day back in England. As the mist cleared, the shade lifted and the boys stood motionless in an unfamiliar place, a place called Dornachrov.

Chapter 4
The Dornachs

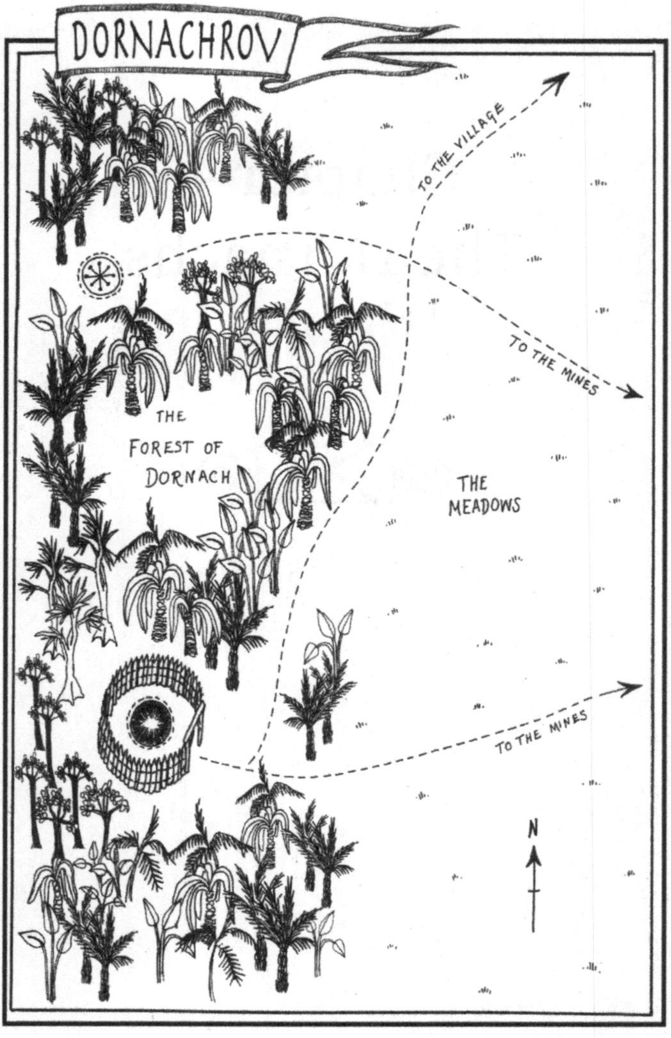
DORNACHROV
TO THE VILLAGE
TO THE MINES
THE FOREST OF DORNACH
THE MEADOWS
TO THE MINES
N

They stood silent, fearful of moving, gazing around at this strange place. Unfamiliar vegetation, giant ferns, tree creeper vines reaching down from tall canopies. *Was this some kind of rainforest* Thought Tom, the air was humid and the ground covered in thick, damp undergrowth, this was not England. They were standing in a large clearing; around the edge a barricade had been formed. A ring of sharpened stakes buried deep pointed inward to keep something penned in. Damien opened the book.

'It's unreadable!'

'What you mean it's unreadable? Check the map!' Tom felt his stomach flutter.

'No, no way,' muttered Damien 'the cross and the circle have parted.'

'Let's find better cover and take a proper look.'

Ahead of them there was an opening, a pair of rusting gates hung half open. They ran over and cautiously peered through. The fortifications were old and hadn't been maintained in years.

'This place must have been a fort at some point in time, and that means someone lives around here.' Tom scanned around, in shock at the thought of what had just happened. 'We need to get out before we get spotted.'

The barricade was an earth mound about two meters high. Through the gates lay a track heading into the forest, the boys bolted out and into cover away from the track. Damien checked the markings on the map, the cross had moved and showed accurately their position, just outside of the fort.

'Ok, I don't think it's very far to the circle' Damien studied the map 'but we don't know what the terrain is like.'

'The thought of getting caught by a farmer was bad enough' added Tom 'who knows what these folk could be!'

'Vikings!' Declared Damien.

'Vikings?' Tom whispered 'Where the hell did you pull Vikings from?'

'That fort looks Viking-ish, I saw a book once in the library.'

'Yeah, like you ever visited the library!'

'Piss off I go a lot, I might even get a membership card.'

'You mean you're not actually a member; you just go to the library?'

'Yes, and they have a book on Vikings, and that looks like it was built by them.'

'Then I take it all back, let's hope they don't find us and pillage us or whatever.' Tom sniggered.

'Yeah, they do that.' Added Damien, nervously.

'Oh man, point out a direction and let's move.'

Damien indicated the way, the two of them took a deep breath, and ran. Clumsily they bounded down the track, sounds of a strange world around them responded to their presence. Croaks and shrieks of wild animals echoed out from unseen places, a heavy rustle from surrounding cover startled them. It was slippery and muddy; damp undergrowth filled the air with a heady aroma. The place was alive with strange wildlife curious of these newcomers to their world. They stumbled hastily along, becoming ever more aware that they may not be alone. Pausing to check the map, they were on track. 'I think somebody is watching us.' Tom whispered.

'Let's speed up the pace then, Vikings won't catch us!'

Damien set off faster, closely followed by Tom. The rough track gradually became steeper, harder for them to keep their footing on the wet ground. Tom slipped, slushing and skidding down the hill on his backside taking Damien with him like a domino. Feet first the pair slid down hill bumping, yelping and splashing to a muddy stop at the bottom. They sat for a moment, dishevelled and feeling a little stupid.

'My bad.' Said Tom, laughing at the state of them both.

'Mum's gonna kill us.' Laughed Damien.

'Welcome to Dornachrov!' The boys, muddy, shocked and a little bruised looked around anxiously, but saw no one. 'There's nothing to be afraid of here, the Dornachs are a peaceful race.'

'We don't mean you any harm, we...' before Tom could finish, a tall, slim figure stepped out of the undergrowth.

'Vikings! Told you!' Whispered Damien.

'Shut up you idiot.'

'It's alright, get your breath back, you have nothing to be afraid of here, are you hurt?' Said the figure.

'I don't think so.' replied Tom.

'Then come with me, the least we can do is offer you hospitality.' Before them stood the tall, slim figure of a man dressed in medieval garb, a brown leather waistcoat, trousers and brown leather boots. Around his waist a leather belt with a short sword attached to his left side. 'I am Ronat, Warrior Chief of Dornachrov' He announced 'and this is Morraine, Warrior Sergeant of Dornachrov.' A broader, older figure stepped out from the cover of a fern. Morraine had a thick beard which underlined two rosy cheeks, had he not been dressed as a warrior, he could have passed for a gentle grandfather sort, with a warm, broad smile. Morraine was formidable, a man you would want as your friend or bodyguard, not your enemy. Around his waist was strapped a thick leather belt, and from this, hung a sabre.

'It has been a long time since that book has travelled, in which land did you find it?' Enquired Morraine, in a deep gravelled voice.

'Erm, we only found it yesterday.' replied Tom, his voice

shaking, revealing his fear inside.

'I am Damien and this is Tom, we're from England, where did you say we are again?'

'This is Dornachrov, and that explains why you look so surprised to see us.' chuckled Morraine, the two boys nervously laughed along, relieved at meeting someone so welcoming, yet weary of what was ahead of them.

'Let's get you two cleaned up and fed, looks like you could both do with a good feeding' Morraine patted his round pot belly and laughed again 'plenty of good food in Dornachrov.'

Welcoming though Dornachrov was, it was far from home, and Tom realised they were now reliant on Ronat and Morraine. Unaware of what lay ahead, this was not a comforting thought, yet he knew they had little choice but to go along with it.

Ronat led the group through the forest with Morraine at the rear. More like a rainforest than your typical English woodland, tall trees held a thick canopy above, providing shelter from the Sun. The air was warm and humid with a strange earthy aroma about it, unfamiliar insects and birds darted and fluttered by. This was not a place they wanted to spend the night. The path was overgrown and hadn't seen much use, but the forest began to thin out, and through the thinning tree trunks a meadow could be seen beyond. Tall meadow grass baked under the heat of the sun, stretching for miles in each direction. A track crossed the meadow ahead of them, Ronat led the party onto it and through a gentle, upward sloping valley. In the distance beyond a shallow rise, fine needles of smoke rose gracefully skyward, piercing the faintest of clouds.

'That's where we're heading.' Ronat pointed to the thin lines of smoke, it was too far to make out inhabitants or even houses at this distance, but slowly, as they reached the brow of a hill, the whole village came into view.

'It looks medieval.' Damien gasped in awe at the sight. Tiny rows of wooden houses lined narrow lanes, small square patches of open ground where children played. Square buildings, round huts, all of different shape and size, maze-like in appearance.

'When we arrive, you will need to meet with the Elder' It's customary for visitors to be received into the village.' Morraine advised, wiping sweat from his brow on a rag of a handkerchief. 'Nothing to be afraid of, she's a kind old soul.' His deep gravelled voice brought a calming presence, as he lumbered along behind the group.

They walked on through the meadow grass and joined a cart track. As they made their way through the fields, villagers working the land looked on at the two strangers. Morraine would wave and call out to friends, occasionally updating the boys on various aspects of fauna.

'Now that's a Maryboat Mallow, you can eat those, very sweet and tasty, that's how I made this.' Morraine patted his belly and laughed. 'Ah now that one's a Braggen Claw Root. Don't eat that, don't even touch it! It'll burn your skin quick as a branding iron that will.'

Tom and Damien listened in awe at their new found teacher, Morraine seemed to know everything about everything here.

The farm hands were dressed in simple clothes, medieval in appearance, each pausing from their work to observe the newcomers, as the group passed through the farm fields. Approaching the village, it was far bigger than they first thought. No longer a mosaic of shapes and colours, it consisted of wooden buildings spread out over several acres, each dwelling of a different shape and size to its neighbour. Some of the buildings were quite substantial two-story houses, while others took the shape of simple round huts. The sound of a blacksmith's hammer chimed out on the far side of the village, and at the centre there appeared to be a square with a roundhouse beyond. By now, some of the villagers had left their work in the fields and started to follow the group along the track. Ronat led them towards the roundhouse. Wood smoke and animal dung filled the air with stench as a growing procession followed on behind. Just outside the door to the roundhouse Ronat stopped and turned to the boys.

'You should wait here while I speak with the Elder.' He ducked inside the house leaving the boys outside with Morraine. Quite a crowd had formed, a friendly bunch, but this didn't help calm the nerves. The boys were far from home and beginning to feel like part of a sideshow. Morraine chatted and joked with some of the farm workers, everyone knew him, he was well respected here, and the local folk felt safe around him.

'You can come in now.' Said a voice from inside the hut, Ronat was holding open a thick animal skin curtain that served as a door.

Tom ducked inside and Damien followed. It was a large round hut, and even though the ceiling was high, a choking stench of wood smoke, herbs and spices filled the air with a sickly-sweet odour. A fire burned in the centre of the earthen floor, but other than that, the boys could see nothing else at first. Their eyes being unaccustomed to the dark made it difficult to see as they scanned around, eyes squinting to identify any shape they could make out. Maybe they were alone; maybe they had to wait here for the Elder, then slowly, as their eyes adjusted, they realised they were not alone.

Chapter 5
A Favour

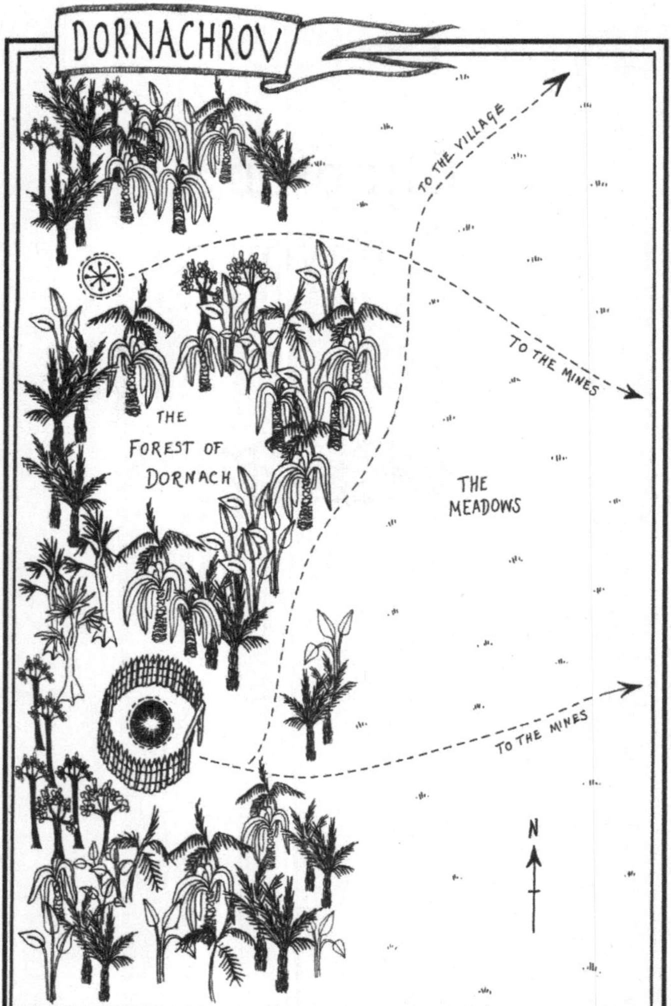
DORNACHROV
TO THE VILLAGE
TO THE MINES
THE FOREST OF DORNACH
THE MEADOWS
TO THE MINES
N

All around the walls of the hut were shelves and racks filled with jars and boxes. Strings of herbs hung down from the roof, blackened cooking pots stacked crooked beside the fire. Beyond the fire stood a bench with a scattering of knives and implements upon it. Hunched over the bench, peering into a book, stooped an old woman.

'So, you have the missing book of Cregheligan?' She croaked, 'It has not returned to Dornachrov for many years, many things will change because of this journey, many, many things will change now.' The old woman did not look up, she carried on with her work, mixing, chopping and stirring a concoction. She paused occasionally to squint upon a book propped up on the bench. Then she stopped and turned, observing the boys for the first time, knife in hand she pointed.

'To what purpose do you intend to use this book, for good or for bad?' asking the question threateningly.

'We didn't mean to use it, we had no idea we could travel with it, but we won't use it for bad reasons.' blurted Tom, clumsily.

'That book is one of three, it was sent away to save our lands and others from invasion, sit down, you should know and understand what powers that book holds.'

The Elder rubbed her hands together then wiped them on her apron. Moving closer to the fire, the boys sat together on a small wooden bench. Shuffling over to a low stool the old woman pulled a pipe from the pouch around her waist and bent forward. Taking a burning twig from the fire, she offered the flame up to the pipe, then began to puff life into its contents. The pipe glowed, dimly at first until a bright orange flare lit up the woman's face more clearly. Coughing out a cloud of smoke she spat to the side of the fire, then wiping her mouth sat down.

'The three books of Cregheligan were written a long

time ago in a land called Cregheligan. The people, known as the Creghelt, were a clever race, they learned the ways of old magic and inner sight, a way of communicating through the senses.' The woman drew hard on the pipe again, as if to pull the story from its embers. She paused to savour the taste then puffed out a plume of white smoke. 'The Creghelt created three books to allow them to travel through time and space, the focus of their work was to bring peace, teach and learn throughout time and eternity.'

The Elder paused and stared into the fire. Watching as the amber flames lapped upwards, curling and wrapping themselves around the burning logs. She took three short puffs on her pipe keeping its glow awake, then reached over to the blackened pot above the fire. Ladling out three mugs of hot steamy liquid, she offered one to each boy and took one for herself. Pursing her wrinkled lips she blew across the top.

'Each book opens a passage through time and space using lands as stepping-stones to other lands. These books have not been used in a long time; the book changes its language to suit the holder, but only becomes readable within the passing circle.' She paused again, blowing the top of her mug before taking a sip, wincing at the heat of the brew.

'There is a map inside the cover which is always readable. Ten pages follow, the first nine pages will take you to different lands, but the last page will always take you back from where you came. No one knows how many lands there are. New lands appear as you journey through each, the journeys seem endless. But, if one of the three books is lost without a keeper, then all three books lose their power until that one is found again.' She puffed again at the pipe and took a sip from the brew. 'You are now the keepers of this book until you pass it on, or it is taken by force. You can, of course, send the book away to be lost. You do this by laying the book on the ground and without touching it you read the passage on the final page. If you do this you will be trapped in that world for the rest of your days, or until the book is found again.' The elder took sip of the brew, then re-lit her fading pipe with another ember from the fire.

Damien gave Tom a side glance to see if he would take a drink first, seeing no indication of movement, Damien raised the mug to his lips and cautiously tasted a little, the liquid tasted like tea, but sweet with a strong earthy flavour about it, not at all unpleasant.

'So, by finding this book we have brought the others back to life?' asked Tom.

'You have indeed, which begs another question, when will the Yarromites realise that their book has regained its powers, and how will they choose to use it this time?' The Elder pointed her pipe at Tom. 'You see, had the Creghelt folk kept hold of all three books there wouldn't be a problem. Unfortunately, one of the books fell into the hands of the Yarromites.' The Elder shook her head. 'The Yarromites were an evil race, they stole a book from one of the Creghelt elders. They then used that book to invade and raid other lands. It took some time for the Creghelt to find out what had happened, but when they did, they sent one of the remaining books away without a keeper. It was expected to be lost for ever, but now you have brought them back to life once more.' The Elder leaned back, and looking into the fire took a few shallow puffs on her pipe.

The boys remained silent, staring into the fire with a faint look of apprehension across their faces.

'If this book was the lost one, then the others could still be in someone else's possession, and they could start to travel. So, if one is sent away while we are travelling, we are stuck here?' Tom nervously added.

'It's not quite that simple, the books are bound to the land they were created in, and that land is Cregheligan. A book can only be sent away from that land. You two have a gift, a gift that should be used carefully and with respect, but nevertheless it is a gift and it was made to be used.' The woman stood up and walked over to the bench 'I have a favour to ask.' she announced while bunching together some herbs. 'There is a place known as Magellion, where a plant grows that cannot grow anywhere else, it can be found on the upper plains quite close to the passing circle. I know, I have been there myself many years ago.' She wrapped a string around the bunched herbs and tied them together tightly. 'The plant cures the sick and prolongs life, if you can fetch some to me, I would be indebted to you.'

'We would be glad to.' Announced Tom without thinking of any potential consequences. Damien felt his stomach tighten as Tom exercised his habit of diving in head first to please others.

'Your friend doesn't look so enthusiastic, are you sure you want to do this?'

'Oh no, it's not that, I just wondered how long it might take? We'll be in trouble if we're not home by 9 o'clock.' said Damien.

'Ah, you are worried about time.' The old woman smiled. 'When the book travels for the first time, the time in your home land stands still for its keepers. So, no matter how long you stay away from home, the moment you leave will be the moment you return, but only the first time the book is used. It was almost written with you in mind.' The old woman smiled a warm and toothless gesture, a little unnerving to observe. 'I will ask Ronat to set up a small camp at the old fort for when you return. We need to make sure that you get back to the village safely.' The Elder pulled open a heavy wooden drawer beneath the bench, taking out a single blue flower she handed it to Damien. 'You will need to know what to look for, we have very few stocks of this plant left and what we do have are dried, the plant flowers blue all year round and can be found on the uppermost plains of Magellion. It is, as far as I know, the only blue flowering plant in the land. I shall send four villagers with you to help, but take care, it has been many years since I was last in Magellion, things might have changed. Ronat!'

'Yes Elder!'

'Take the boys and prepare them for the passing circle, along with four of our warriors, they have agreed to fetch us some Eldwitch herb.'

'Eldwitch, but can't that only be found on Magellion?' asked Ronat.

'Yes, that's where they will find it, now take them to prepare for their journey, and have a small camp set up at the old fort for when they return.'

'Yes Elder.'

Ronat led the boys outside, Morraine had left and most of the farm workers had returned to their fields. Across the square stood a large wooden house, the front door was a thick, rough wooden affair, battered and worn from heavy use. Ronat pushed it open leading them into a kitchen, a log fire burned within a brick fireplace, an iron hook on a chain dangled down over the fire with a pot hanging from it. The smell of woodsmoke and stew combined to give off a wholesome touch to the place. A rustic wooden bench and dining table stood in the centre of the room, on the table rested several goblets, a jug of water and a wooden box. The boys sat on the bench and took off their rucksacks, still caked with dried mud from their unceremonious arrival.

'Ronat.' Asked Tom.

'Yes.'

'You sounded surprised at the Elder's request to travel to Magellion? Have you been there before?'

'No, I have not, but you must take care, there are stories from long ago about that place, keep one eye on the skies at all times. Now wait here while I find some volunteers, help yourself to food and water.'

Damien looked inside the box, and took out a small bread cob. 'Are you sure this is a smart move?' He asked, breaking off a piece of the soft bread.

'No, I think it's a pretty stupid move, but imagine if we go home now. Imagine waking up tomorrow and never knowing. Imagine trying to live a regular life after giving up on the greatest adventure we could ever have dreamt of.'

'I don't get it though, Ronat didn't see the book, we didn't mention it, but he knew we had travelled with it.'

Tom took some bread from the box. 'It does feel strange, like they were waiting for us.'

'I don't know, we might be over thinking it, but I think the Elder has some kind of special power.' Mumbled Damien through a mouthful. 'This bread is amazing by the way, and that's not a sentence I've ever used before.' He chuckled, dark and sweet, the bread looked more like fruitcake, but with a rich honey-like taste. It stuck to the mouth as it slowly melted to a sweet, creamy texture.

Tom nodded almost hypnotised by the flavour, then poured them both a goblet of water, completely forgetting what they were just talking about.

They began to dry off their clothes by the fire, brushing off crusted mud as Ronat arrived with four young men.

'Tom, Damien, these are your helpers, Dodrill, Tumalle, Samian and Gorlish.' The newcomers smiled and nodded, dressed similar to Ronat in leather waistcoats and coarse fabrics, the six of them exchanged greetings.

'Have you been to Magellion before?' asked Dodrill taking a seat at the table.

'No, coming here was the first time we travelled with the book.' Replied Tom.

'Mother said there are Braggens there,' replied Dodrill 'Huge bird-like beasts with giant claws.'

'Your mother also said there was a two headed bear in the forest, as tall as a tree, who ate children.' Gorlish laughed, the others joined in, as they each began to tear off pieces of bread.

'Oh she said that to stop us going into the forest, but it's true about the Braggens! That's how the old village was lost, the Braggens took them all.' Dodrill replied stuffing a small chunk of bread in his mouth. 'Oh this bread, Herran is the best baker in Dornachrov, I'll marry her one day.'

'She wouldn't have you, not with those stinking feet!' Samian joined in the banter.

'My feet don't stink!'

'My mum said they could smell you before you were even born!' Tumalle added. The kitchen erupted in laughter as they shared food and drink.

Ronat smiled and slipped into the back room of the house, he returned with a cloth-wrapped package placing it on a wooden chest with a clatter. Tom and Damien turned around.

'You should take these, they might come in useful for clearing your path.' He unwrapped the cloth, on the table lay two short swords attached to two leather belts. Damien picked one up and examined it. The belt and scabbard were tatty and worn, but the blade carried a sharp edge.

Wrapping the leather belts around their waist they fastened them tight. The weapons slung heavy, but offered some comfort in their weight, a sense of protection.

When all six of them had finished chatting and eating, Ronat took them outside and introduced them to Doon. Doon was a Warrior Sergeant of Dornachrov, he stood tall and slim with a fresh complexion. A bow hung from his shoulder, and a quiver of arrows slung low about his waist. His eyes, piercing aqua blue, with a look of intelligence about him.

Ronat and Doon led the group back the way they came towards the forest.

'It's quite a walk to the circle' Ronat announced as he walked briskly ahead 'but don't worry, no mud slides to contend with this time.' The boys laughed, clothes still damp and crusty from their unceremonious arrival.

Like a band of warriors going off to battle, Ronat carrying his spear with a short sword on his belt, Doon with his bow, then six swordsmen tagged on to the rear. Each adventurer had been given a shoulder bag containing sacks for the flowers, a small packet of fruit bread and a skin of water for the journey. The shoulder bags helped Tom and Damien counter-balance the sword and scabbard worn around their waist. Neither felt too sure about the gift or why they might need such a thing, but it made them feel equal in a strange world, and thought it polite to accept the offer.

On entering the forest, Ronat led them along a track which branched off to the right, it weaved its way uphill between ancient trees and thick, earthy scented vegetation. Although it was only midday, the light was dim due to the leafy green canopy obscuring most of the sunlight. This canopy helped keep the forest cool, and in doing so gave it an eerie touch. Here and there razor-sharp shards of sunlight pierced through, slicing down to the bed of undergrowth beneath. There was a strong, potent smell of wild garlic as they approached a narrow foot bridge. Clobbering over the old timber planks they crossed a small stream, picking up the track beyond. The path traversed a wooded valley as they slowly progressed uphill.

'The Elder tells me you travelled from a land known as England?' Doon asked.

'Yes, have you been there?' Replied Tom.

'No, but I have heard tales of it from long ago.'

'Really! So, people have travelled there in the past?'

'Oh yes, there are many tales of many lands. Folk sometimes left their own lands to move to others, the Elder is one of those folk.'

'The Elder has travelled?'

'Yes, she is much older than she looks, that's what the Eldwitch herb is for.' Replied Doon.

The path grew narrower as Ronat led the group to the entrance of a small clearing. 'This is as far as we can take you, and so I'll wish you good luck!'

Tom turned to find Damien retrieving the book from his pack, as one by one the group edged their way into the centre of the clearing. He turned to Ronat 'Thanks for showing us the way, we'll see you soon.'

Ronat smiled 'We will be waiting for you at the old fort where you arrived.' Ronat nodded, turned and stepped back with Doon to a safer distance.

Re-slinging his shoulder pack, Damien gazed around at the passing circle, then opened the book. The pages were now readable, and turning to the page titled "Magellion" he held up the book and paused to take a breath, Damien began to recite a now familiar phrase.

'Elders of the book of Cregheligan,
we seek channel to Magellion,
through worlds afar,
part the elements,
part time and space,
through the void of existence grant this journey.'

Chapter 6
Yarromovia

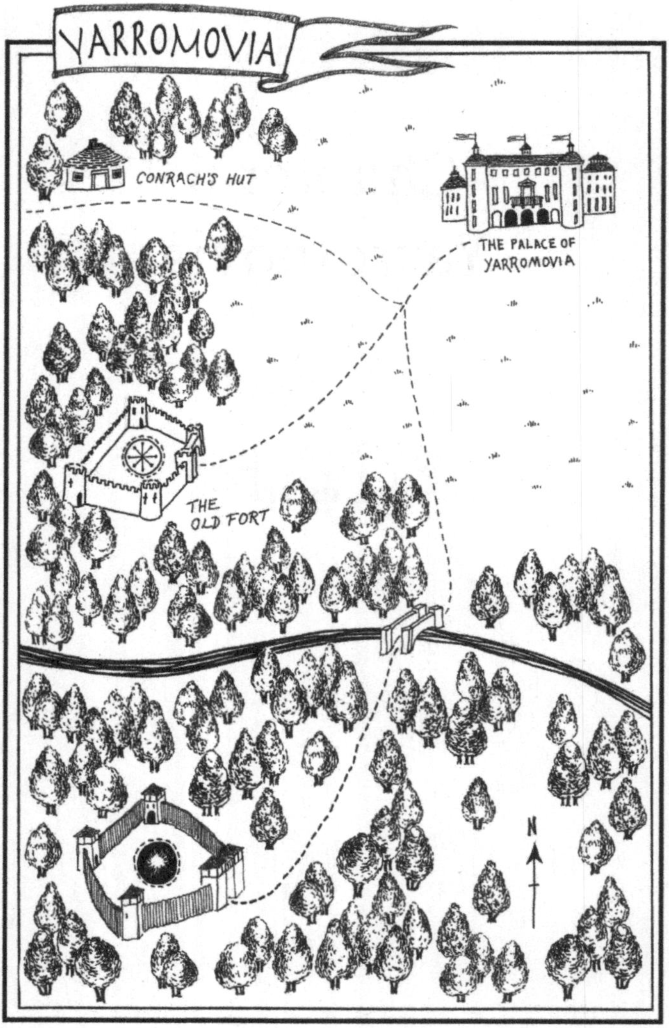
YARROMOVIA
CONRACH'S HUT
THE PALACE OF
YARROMOVIA
THE
OLD FORT
N

Squelching through muddy puddles. Conrach, an Elder of the Yarromites huffed and panted, slipping and stumbling towards the Grand Imperial City. Under his left arm was tucked a leather satchel, old and battered yet he clung to it as if his own life depended on it. Before him towered grey stone walls, speckled with arrow slits enclosing the city. Guards evenly placed along the battlements, quietly motionless observing the outer lands. Conrach scurried on like a rat, following the line of the cobbled city road. The sweet sickly smell of rotting flesh and sewerage growing stronger as he grew closer. Had he looked up from the road he would have seen the grey silhouettes, corpses encased in creaking gibbets, teased by the wind. Conrach kept his eyes fixed on the path ahead, rain seeping through the shoulders of his cloak, cold and damp. Thinking, scurrying, muttering anxiously to himself through the blackness of night, as corpses hung around him.

Approaching the steps to the walled city two guards edged forward lowering spears.

'Out of my way! Don't you recognise your Elder?' Conrach barked as he hurried towards them, the guards snatched back their weapons and stood upright at once. Conrach, sweating and panting even heavier, hurriedly made his way through the outer portcullis gates and along the broad cobbled street. Stepping out onto the Square of the Emperors, with the palace looming in the distance. White marbled stone carved thousands of years ago and still as pristinely white as the day it was first laid. Silver spired towers embellishing each corner of the palace reached high above the ramparts. Shimmering wet with rain as torchlight reflected off the glass-like smoothness. Lined between the upper layers of stonework, thin trimmings of silver glistened as rainwater polished over.

Conrach crossed the square, by now the stench beyond the outer wall had faded into a pleasing aroma of sweet floral incense. Faint smoke plumes gently wafted through the square. Placed evenly within cloisters, hanging censers swung gracefully around the edge of the palace walls. Climbing the steps of the palace, Conrach approached a huge arched doorway. Two thick oak doors towered before him, and in the centre, a wicket gate. Conrach banged hard on it, within seconds a wary eye appeared through the square grill of an observation hatch, it slammed shut and the door opened. Conrach heaved up his wet cloak and squeezed his way through.

'I need to see the Emperor at once; it is of the upmost importance'.

Cautiously looking Conrach over, the palace guard ushered him forward.

'Please Elder, follow me.'

Conrach followed, unbuttoning the chain of his cloak, he slipped it from his shoulders and threw it at a nearby servant. The guard led the way through oak panelled, marble floor corridors, his pike staff over his shoulder. Steel studded boots clicked sharply on the floor with every step, complimenting a finely fitted crimson and black tunic. The tunic was embellished with silver buttons together with knee-length black leather boots and silver spurs, all suggesting an air of authority and superiority. On reaching the end of a long corridor they turned and entered a large ornate room. Portraits and battle scenes hung from the walls, ancestors, living and dead. The ceiling, decorated with a finely painted hunting scene, all went unnoticed as the guard presented Conrach to the Emperor's aide. The guard turned sharply and left the room.

'I have important news for the Emperor!'

'I believe the Emperor is resting at the moment Sir, can it wait a while?'

'I must see him right now, he will understand.'

'Very well Sir, this way please.'

They entered an adjoining room, carved wooden panels stretched from floor to ceiling, a comforting whiff of beeswax filled the air. Heavy, leather clad furniture was set out, huddled together in small clusters. The aide pointed to a chair beside the fireplace, standing impatiently beside it, Conrach took a moment to dry his clothes discretely. Making his way to the far end of the room the aide spoke softly to a servant. The servant nodded then slipped quietly through a nearby doorway. Conrach fumbled with the bindings of his satchel, steam rising from the warmth of the fire at his back. A damp odour combined with sweat began to seep through his layers of clothing and sour the room. Conrach waited, fumbling and muttering and stinking, the door opened again.

'His Imperial Majesty will see you now Sir, if you would kindly follow me?'

Conrach hurried over to the doorway still fumbling with the satchel, following the servant through they entered a large antechamber. Two Imperial guards stood before a double doorway, the servant braced himself and with a sharp knock the door opened.

'Conrach the Elder my Lord.' Conrach stepped through bowing awkwardly. The Emperor stood beside his writing desk, facing a narrow glass window overlooking his private gardens as lanterns flickered their amber glow around its trellised walls. Tall and thinly built, a fine black velvet dressing gown hung from his narrow shoulders, almost touching the floor.

'Whenever you enter my chambers Conrach you bring either very good news or very bad. Which is it this time?'

'My Lord, please forgive the intrusion.' Conrach pulled a tatty leather book from his satchel and placed it on the desk beside the emperor. 'I hereby deliver to you the book of Cregheligan. It is readable once more my Lord!'

The emperor turned sharply and glared down at the book. 'Guards!'

A hidden door in the corner of the room burst open, two Royal body guards stood, their hands poised to draw swords. 'Send for the Commander in Chief immediately!'

'Yes your Majesty.' The guards acknowledged and quickly left the room. The emperor turned to Conrach.

'This is indeed good news; in fact, it is the best news you have ever brought me Conrach.' He leant forward stroking a bony hand across the damp cover, in stark contrast to its elegant surroundings. 'Is it likely the Creghelt will send away their last book?'

'It is impossible to say my Lord, if they do then they have no way of ever regaining control of all three books again.' Conrach anxiously rubbed his hands. 'I am quite sure they never anticipated the book being found, and I am certain they could not live with the thought of their final creation being lost and found again.' Conrach laughed nervously.

'In that case let us make the most of it while we can.' The emperor paused, 'Forgive me, you must cold, please warm yourself by the fire.' Taking a small bell from the desk he rang and another door opened. 'Tea and fruit-bread at once!'

'Yes your Majesty.' The servant bowed and backed out of the room gracefully.

The Emperor picked up the book, wincing at the dampness he placed it back. A knock at the door.

'The Commander in Chief my Lord!'

'Burwell! Come in! I have a mission for you.'

'Yes, my Lord?' The Commander glanced at the Elder

who was now sitting smugly in a large leather chair by the fire. Conrach heaved himself up from the chair and shuffled over.

'Do you know what this is Commander?' Gesturing towards the book, Conrach continued. 'It is the gateway to wealth, to riches and to victory. It holds power greater than you could ever imagine. It has rested for many years and now it has awakened!'

Squinting down at the book, the Commander then turned to the Emperor.

'What this old fool is trying to say, is that I wish for you to assemble my armies. We will need both defensive and offensive forces, raiding parties, slave masters, logistics. Burwell, we are going to war!'

The Commanders jaw dropped slightly.

'I, I am not sure I even begin to understand my Lord. We have conquered all of our lands and oppressed all opposition. Are there rebellions that I'm not aware of?'

'No Burwell, forgive me.' The Emperor turned, pacing with grandeur, gesturing eccentrically as if addressing his Empire. 'This book is not of this world, it has powers that only the Elders can truly understand, but you' he pointed 'together with Conrach, are about to experience all of these. I hereby gift to you both, the Book of Cregheligan.' The last sentence causing Conrach's spine to tingled with excitement.

'Conrach will explain, but for now I want you to assemble a small reconnaissance party, no more than half a dozen Royal guards. Between yourself and Conrach choose somewhere safe, and experience the secrets of this book.' The Emperor looked down at the damp, weathered book on the desk. 'Do not draw attention to yourselves gentlemen, we have more important tasks ahead, just bring back something nice!' The Emperor rang the small bell again and the servant entered. 'Good luck gentlemen.'

Conrach led Burwell out of the Royal chambers and down the Palace steps. Guiding his bewildered guest through the cold dampness of night to an alleyway left of the Square. They squelched their way through streets and lanes until reaching a doorway with the word "Apothecary" carved in stone above. Pulling a large iron key from his pocket, Conrach fumbled it into the keyhole. The door groaned as he turned the key and pushed it open, revealing a large room covered in a blanket of dust. Taking out a small tinderbox from his satchel, he slid open the lid and placed it on a long wooden table in the centre of the room. A room which hadn't been used in years, and when it was, it was never used as an apothecary.

Reaching over, Conrach dragged a candlestick from the centre of the table. He took the flint and steel from his tinderbox, then lifted the damper revealing a char cloth beneath. Conrach struck down hard several times with the flint until a spark lit the char cloth causing a rich orange firefly glow. He placed the tip of a brimstone match against it and blew, the match ignited. Conrach lit the candle, cupping the flame and guiding Burwell to the back of the room they began to descend a narrow spiral stairwell.

The air, stale and damp, cobweb netted corners sparked into flame with a kiss from the candle as it passed. Moving along the cobblestone passage, passing closed doors on either side. This place was vast; Burwell's curiosity grew *how did I not know about this?* He stayed within the bubble of light cast by Conrach's candle as more doorways came into view then disappeared into the abyss behind them.

'Here we are.' Conrach muttered. Placing a hand on the rusty iron latch Conrach turned and pushed, it failed to move. Burwell shouldered the door scraping it half open. Inside, Conrach shuffled around and began to light candles until the whole room glowed with an amber warmth about it. As before, dust covered everything, bookshelves lined the walls, a line of writing bureaus stood unused for decades. Burwell scanned the room, this was an operations room, a room where raids and invasions were planned and directed.

'As the Commander in Chief I should know about this, yet it's all new to me. Why wasn't I made aware of this place?' Burwell slowly paced around the room 'Conrach, what is this place?'

Conrach turned his attention to a large map chest, holding the candlestick he bent forward, squinting in the dim light he read out the markings.

'a, b, c, d!'

The chest was formed of several long narrow drawers, each labelled alphabetically.

'This, Commander, was the former centre of operations for Yarromovia, here take this.' Conrach offered the candlestick to Burwell, he then pulled gently on the drawer marked "D" and taking out an old tattered map he placed it on the table.

'From this room raids were planned and executed, maps drawn up of new worlds and the Empire of Yarromovia was formed.' Burwell watched and listened in amazement. 'When the powers of that book ceased, there was no need for all of this, but there was also no need to make anyone aware of it either, secrecy is the key, Commander.'

The map's edges were feathered and brown, with the name "Devlon" inscribed at the top. Several islands were delicately drawn on the parchment, a circle in red, and a cross in blue.

'This is where we shall arrive,' Conrach pointed to the cross 'and this is where we leave.' a thick, ink-stained finger slid across the parchment to the circle.

'And what manner of people can we expect to find in this land?' asked Burwell.

'These people are basic folk, more focused on drinking and sleeping than anything else. We should be able to slip in and out unnoticed. But if we are noticed I doubt we shall encounter warriors.'

'Then it sounds perfect for a training exercise, I'll have an escort prepared. When would you like to leave?'

'I'll need some time to plan, we cannot afford to lose this book on our first mission Commander.' Conrach moved over to a small stove and began poking around inside. 'Remember, light weapons for defence only, and simple dress. The purpose of this mission is to test and demonstrate the powers of this book. We are not going to war just yet Commander Burwell.'

Burwell grinned.

'I shall send word when all is ready, you can find your way out I presume?'

'Indeed Elder, I look forward to hearing from you.' Burwell smiled, picked up a candlestick and made his way back down the corridor.

Conrach took some kindling sticks and logs from beside the stove, carefully assembling them inside its firebox, the touch of a candle flame did the rest. The warmth and aroma began to fight against the dampness of the room, bringing a sense of life back into the place. He peered over the map, slowly running his hands across its rough texture.

'I never believed that I would have the world to myself.' Illuminated by candlelight his expression appeared ever more sinister, as his laughter echoed hauntingly along the corridors.

Chapter 7
Magellion

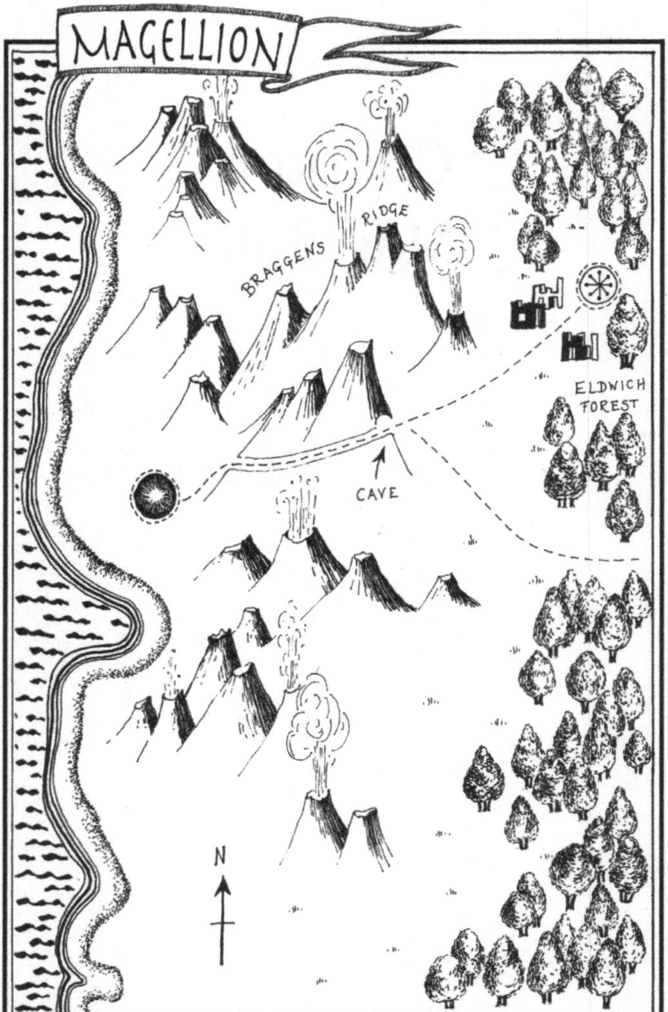
MAGELLION
BRAGGENS RIDGE
ELDWICH FOREST
CAVE
N

A shade fell upon the area, cold and deathly. The ground began to vibrate just as before, soil levitating as it bounced to the frequency of vibrations. The six adventurers lost focus of what was around them, visions blurred as senses mixed reality with dreams. Shade turned to darkness, the scent of a foul, earthy mist filled the air, grasping at lungs, it snatched their world from them. Faces ran in watercolours, blending, swirling into grey for an eternity, or was it just a second. The mist slowly began to clear as the ground beneath them calmed, revealing a world so different from the one they left behind. This world was Magellion.

They found themselves standing in a small, ash covered clearing overlooking a valley. Around them towered mountainous volcanic rocks. The sky was dark with smog, reddened by what lay beneath. A landscape, craggy and volcanic, sliced apart by crawling rivers of lava. Crimson ribbons of fire, snaking their way through a gigantic canyon. Lava flows slid by gracefully, puffing pillows of smoke into the air. Air, the stench of sulphur, hot and unpleasant. They stood in awe at the sight before them.

'Where the hell are we!' Damien gasped.

'The map, show me the map.' Replied Tom scanning the smoke-filled skies above them.

Damien, handed over the book. There was no greenery to be seen at all, the group had arrived at the foot of a steep craggy rockface stretching upward into a soot filled sky. A sky obscured by cushions of thick, dense cloud. The heat was unbearable as the six of them looked around. In the distance, two large birds could be seen gliding on set wings, gracefully weaving between mountain peaks.

'Keep an eye on the skies.' Recalled Damien as he watched.

'Braggens!' Dodrill added.

They hid their fear well, as Tom opened the book and studied the map. The deep valley was clearly marked on the page, with the lava flows stretching through it. It was hard to distinguish the terrain, but the passing circle lay above them, beyond the craggy rocks on which they found themselves perched.

'It's not good, we have some climbing to do.' Tom sighed, pointing in the general direction of the circle.

'Let's get started, there's a bit of a track up here.' Damien adjusted his pack and set off for the track. It was steep and uneven, just wide enough for one person at a time.

The ground, crunching with each gravelly step, scrambling they followed the track up hill and away from the lava flow. Grabbing onto warm rocks either side to steady themselves as they climbed. It felt hot beneath their feet as clouds of strong sulphurous gasses wafted about them, filling the air with an odour of rotten eggs. Gravel and ash sweeping away from beneath them as hand-over-hand they clung on to the rocks, pushing and pulling ahead. Sweat dripped from Tom's nose as he paused to look up *how much farther*.

Ahead, the track zigzagged as it curved its way higher, navigating the steep incline towards the mouth of a cave. The entrance grew wider and wider as they approached.

'The Elder never told us about this!' Tom laughed.

'That old woman never climbed this hill I'm sure of that!' Damien replied, causing a ripple of laughter among the group.

Tom reached the broad flat opening to the cave, took out his torch and shone it inside, darkness. A distant screech echoed out through the canyon behind them.

'What the hell?' Damien yelled.

'Get inside!' screamed Tumalle turning to look down the canyon 'Get in the cave! Get in the cave!' The group scrambled up the remainder of the track, stumbling and slipping on the cinders beneath them. Two huge Dragon-like beasts had seen the torchlight and were approaching. A cloud of dust bellowed into the air as the first Braggen swept past, its claws, like sabres glanced over Damien's back.

'Look out there's another!' cried Tom as he approached the cave entrance, turning to see Dodrill ducking to avoid a second attack. Tom picked up a rock and threw it at the creature while grabbing Samian's hand and dragging him into the blackness. One by one the boys stumbled into the cave.

'Where's Gorlish!' Shouted Tom as Damien, Tumalle and Dodrill collapsed, coughing and choking alongside Samian. Braggens screeched as they swept by outside.

'Gorlish! Gorlish!' there was no reply, Tom made a run for the entrance, but Dodrill grabbed his leg, holding him back within the safety of the cave.

'Stop! It's too late.' Shouted Dodrill.

Tom broke free and stepped outside, there was nothing but clouds of dust. Tom collapsed to his knees exhausted.

'Why didn't she warn us about them?' He shouted, his face now grey with volcanic ash. 'We could have prepared better for this.'

'We wouldn't have come.' Replied Damien. 'Now come inside.'

'I should never have accepted the task; it's my fault your friend is lost.' Tom's eyes welled up with tears, which ran, painting pale streaks through the dust on his cheeks.

'No,' said Dodrill 'we all volunteered to come here, and none of us knew of the danger, it could have been any one of us.' He pulled Tom back into the cave. 'We need to carry on with the mission and get what we came for.' He dusted them both off and took hold of Tom's shoulders, staring him in the face 'Come on, we have to continue.'

In the distance, a feint screech could be heard, followed by another, and then silence.

'So, what happens now? We can't go back that way.' muttered Tom, fixated on the entrance. Damien stared at the entrance for a moment as if searching for an answer.

'Ok, so the track led into the cave, that must mean something, and look,' Damien pointed. 'the smoke, its blowing into the cave too. So, if it's blowing into the cave, it must be coming out somewhere else.'

Tom wiped his face, coughed and spat.

'Ok, but I'm coming back for him.'

The five of them got their things together, still numb with shock they began to desperately fumble their way deeper into the darkness. Switching on the torch Tom looked around. A high, narrow ceiling towered off into the abys above. The passage was just wide enough for one, but far easier going than outside. The cave stank, a sour, damp odour clung to the throat, getting stronger the deeper they travelled. Shuffling and crunching of cinders were the only sounds. The heat of the cave slowed their pace; breathing turned to panting as the air became heavier and harder for lungs to make use of. Continuing steeply upward, a faint screeching sound echoed down from the ceiling, it was too high, too far and too hot to bother with now.

The cave widened and as the path began to level out, a faint touch of cool breeze puffed at their faces. Tom, leading with the torch, stopped and looked around to see the narrow path opening up into a cavern. It was cooler here, and the sound of dripping water echoed through from above.

'Okay, rest here for a few minutes.' said Tom, throwing his pack to one side, his frustration showed. The group gathered round silently and made a small circle. Opening his pack Damien shared out some of the bread, while Tom took one of his water skins, drank and passed it around.

'Are you ok Tom?' asked Damien.

'Yes, but I want to go find him.'

Damien paused, he wanted the same, but now didn't feel like the right time. 'How much further do you think we need to go?'

'I can't tell, but we must be nearing the end,' Replied Tom 'the cave has been getting wider and that cool breeze must mean that we are nearing the top. It's not easy to work out from the map, we've mostly been walking uphill.' He blinked as sweat ran down his brow, washing ash into his eyes. The mood was solemn, they rested and chatted, not noticing the faint twittering and scratching from above. They sharing what food & drink they had, but the mood was sombre. Tom and Damien began to realise that these boys were very similar to the friends they had back home. They had all grown up together, and although they were warriors, they weren't much older than the two of them.

'Gorlishs' death will not go unnoticed, nor will it go unrecognized, his name will live on in our history.' Declared Dodrill. With that the group drank a toast together.

'To Gorlish!' announced Dodrill.

'To Gorlish!' the others repeated, raising their drinks.

Pausing for a moment, they then packed away their things, Tom dusted himself down, and took another look the map. Looking around he checked everyone was ready, then started off through the cave again. The track steepened and the breeze became cooler.

A draft of air wafted down from above, *strange* thought Tom. Then another, and then a screech. He continued, thinking nothing of it, leading the way through the cavern.

Then, as if the ceiling itself were falling in, a whoosh of air blasted past them, screeching and twittering, this wasn't just air. A wave of creatures swirled and screeched around them, swooping and clawing. Too fast to see, shadows of clawing blackness scratched and grabbed at them, sweeping by. A scream went out from one of the party and chaos erupted, ducking and scrambling, frantically trying to get higher up into the cave.

'Damien was that you!' Called out Tom.

'Yes, I've been scratched or bitten or something.'

Tom waved the torch around trying to fend them off. 'Keep going, get out of here.'

Toumale and Samian each grabbed an arm, dragging Damien through the cave beneath the swooping and clawing.

'I can see daylight ahead' shouted Dodrill, 'come on, there's not far to go.'

Dodrill reached the mouth of the cave first, the creatures continued to swoop in the shadows until the last of the group broke through and into daylight. Soot-black and bloody the five of them paused at the mouth of the cave. Toumale examined Damien's face. 'You've been bitten, we need to clean this.'

'In my pack there's a first aid kit.' Damien fumbled for his rucksack.

'Here, let me.' Tom helped 'What happened to you?' Damien's face began to swell, there were several cuts on his face and neck, blood trickled down staining his shirt. Tom opened Damien's rucksack taking out his first aid kit. The kit contained several sticking plasters, antiseptic wipes and some antiseptic cream. Tom set about cleaning and dressing Damien's wounds.

'You'll be ok for now, but we should get help from the Elder when we get back. Wait here.'

Tom crouched, moving cautiously to the mouth of the cave, squinting against the daylight he could see that the cave opened up onto a flat, grassy plateau. To the right, a scattering of shrubs and bushes stretching out to a forest beyond. To the left, the ground sloped off gently into a shallow gorge. There were no signs of life. He looked at the map, then looked around again, calculating which direction they would need to take, *to the left then find a way through the forest to the passing circle.* The skies were empty, there were no Braggens here, but just to be sure he picked out a tree a short distance ahead and made a dash for it. Again, the skies were quiet, there was nothing flying around at all. Tom waited a moment to be sure, then walked back to the entrance of the cave.

'It's okay, it's clear.'

Damien sat, head in hands.

'Are you ok?' Asked Tom.

'I'll be fine, we should keep moving.'

Toumale helped pack away Damien's things as the group prepared to move out. When they had gathered themselves together Tom led the way towards the forest. The scent of rich vegetation filled the air, but still no sign of the blue flowering plant. The going was easy, lush, green grasses, edged by patches of thicket, yet soft underfoot. A faint, lingering smell of sulphurous gas reminded them of the horrors, but this place was different, it felt safer.

Up ahead, broad, ancient tree trunks stretched skyward forming the outer perimeter of a wood. Within its shade they pressed deeper and deeper through a maze of trees, it was hauntingly silent here.

'Wait,' Tom stopped the group 'is that a house?'

The remains of a small stone wall could be seen in the distance; he crouched and moved forward. The ruins of several huts, stood no more than four or five stones tall, covered in moss. Tom waved the rest of the group forward. Then there it was, Dodrill spotted the plant they were looking for, clumped together in small clusters, deep green leaves adorned with bright blue flowers.

'That's it!' He shouted.

The group ran forward, franticly picking and stuffing bright blue flowers into their sacks.

'Take as many as we can carry, the passing circle isn't far from here.' Shouted Tom.

There were thousands beyond the settlement. Taking care not to destroy the plants, they picked and packed their way through them, within thirty minutes all the sacks were full. Plenty more bushes lay untouched, offering a carpet of blue stretching off into the forest.

Tom took out the book and studied the map again, the group gathered round using the ruins of one of the houses to rest in.

'I think it's time to head back to Dornachrov. I'm still not happy about leaving Gorlish behind, we shall come back with more warriors and at least try to find his body.'

With nods and murmurings, the others agreed.

'I will speak to Ronat when we get back,' Said Dodrill 'I feel it's only right that we do this for his mother. Besides, we need to get Damien back to the Elder.'

Tying their sacks they slung them over their shoulders, packed full. Rejoining the track Tom led them off once more. He could feel his leg muscles burn with each step, not so used to this amount of hiking.

They walked on until Tom called a halt within a rocky enclosure. 'This is it, we are standing in the circle.'

Gathering round, damp, sweaty and caked in ash they stood. Tom turned to the last page of the book to find a single line of text which would return them to Dornachrov. 'Merwag ed Wroth'

Chapter 8
Recovery

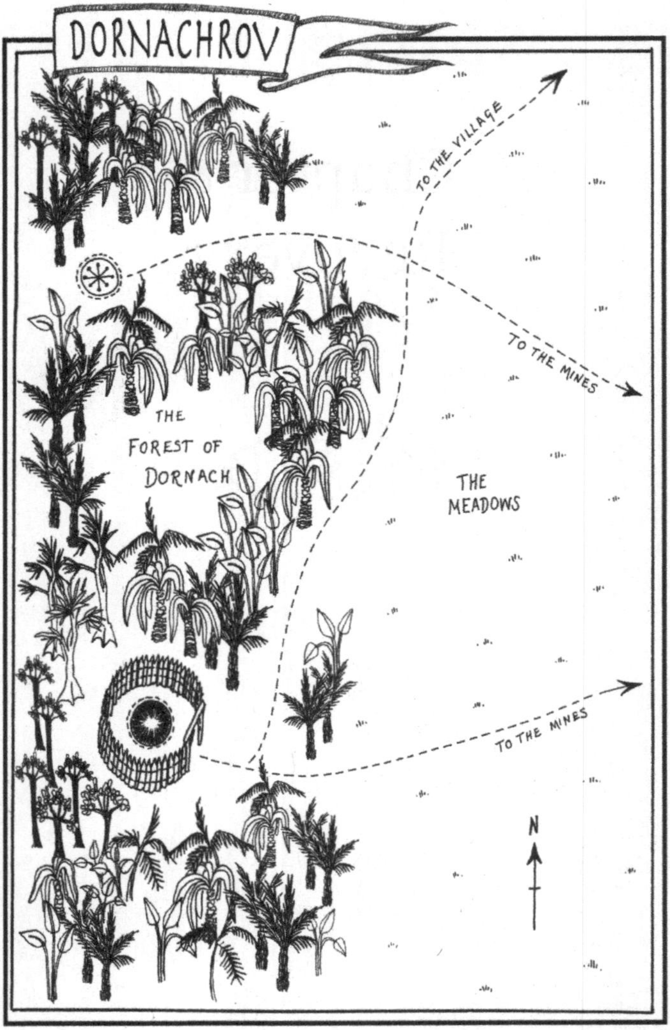
DORNACHROV
TO THE VILLAGE
TO THE MINES
THE FOREST OF DORNACH
THE MEADOWS
TO THE MINES
N

Ronat and Doon sat by a camp fire just beyond the fort barricade, a small band of warriors had joined them, sent by Morraine to help carry the Eldwitch Herb.

'The problem we have now Doon, is that we don't know who or what could come through that gate.' Ronat poked at the fire with a long thin twig. 'Remember when we used to go rock pooling with our grandparents, you would lift the rock and I would wait with the net. We never knew what was under those stones until you turned them, but we always had the net ready.' Ronat placed another log on the embers. 'We need to get that net ready again. Doon, we need to rebuild an army. Dornachrov has had it easy for centuries now, we've grown lazy and accustomed to easy life. The finding of this book will either strengthen us, or destroy us.'

Doon watched as fire lapped over the fresh log. 'I agree, we should speak with the Elder, but we will need help to do this, and we should focus more effort on the mines.'

A low, distant humming noise began, birds lifted up from the trees, flying off in all directions as the ground began to vibrate. The earth shook and a darkness fell upon the area. The warriors tightened their grip on spear and sword, none of them had ever seen this phenomenon before, they were expecting their friends to return, but had no idea what might come through that portal. A haunting mist lifted up from the ground, as the backdrop of forest blurred into liquid form, then they appeared, rushing through and taking a breath of the sweet air of Dornachrov they dropped to the ground exhausted.

'Over here! Is everyone alright? Where's Gorlish, and what happened to your face?' anxiously Ronat scrutinized the party. Damien looked up awkwardly as the bites were beginning to sting and swell.

'We lost him within minutes of arriving, a creature took

him.'

'A creature? Quickly, we need to get you to the Elder, let's see if she can fix you up.' Ronat sent his warriors forward to collect the sacks and help the party.

Doon led the way back through the forest toward the village, while Tom walked with Damien behind Ronat's warriors, the swelling was now making it harder for Damian to see. Ronat walked among them, desperately trying to find out what happened to Gorlish, and what Magellion was like.

'Do you think he could still be alive?' asked Ronat.

'It's hard to tell, those creatures where huge, it must have carried him off.' replied Damien

'Braggens, I'm amazed they exist; I was led to believe it was myth. Had I known I would have sent more warriors. It's my fault, I'm sorry for putting you at such risk.'

This degree of loss was more than either Tom or Damien had ever experienced. Death was always so distant until now, it happens to everyone, they knew that, but neither of them had come so close to it before. Ronat's words were helpful, but they didn't take away the trauma of what had just occurred.

'I can't help thinking we could have done something to prevent this.' muttered Tom.

'Like what? It could have been you or me at the back of that line, it was just bad luck'. said Damin

They walked on through the forest, the place had not changed since the last time they were here. Strange birdsong filled the skies, a familiar earthy smell of undergrowth filled the air, but this time it felt safe.

As they approached the village a small crowd began to form. Fingers pointing in curiosity at the sacks slung over the shoulders of those approaching. Ronat led the group through the square and back to the house where they had all met just a few hours before. Again, food and drink was waiting for them on the table.

'I'll speak with the elder, wait here.' Ronat left, walking back across the square to the Elder's hut.

'Let me take those swords, I doubt you'll need them here.'

Doon collected the swords and took them through to the back room. The boys said nothing, quietly relieved that they didn't have to use them.

'I meant it when I said I want to go back and find him.' Tom said.

'I know you did Tom, and we are coming too.' Replied Dodrill 'We all grew up with him, and we're grateful you are prepared to do this for our friend.'

'But next time we need better torches for that cave.' Added Damien.

'We need fire brands; those things won't attack if we carry flaming torches.' Samian said.

'I don't think you'll be going anywhere soon, you all need to rest, especially you Damien.' Doon said, coming back into the room. 'Besides, there are greater risks to Dornachrov now I fear.'

The door opened and Ronat entered.

'The Elder will see you all when you're ready.'

One by the boys left the house and crossed the square. Tom, Damien, Samian, Dodrill and Tumalle were ushered inside the Elder's hut. She stood, hunched beside the fire in the centre, a young girl stood beside her holding a wooden platter.

'Dornachrov is indebted to you, and one of our own has paid the highest price today. You each volunteered, you offered to take on this task on behalf of Dornachrov, and for your services Dornachrov grants you the freedom of its lands.' The old woman turned to the young girl taking a necklace from the platter. 'Take this charm and wear it always.'

Leaning forward she placed it over Tom's head, he felt the Elder's hand on his shoulder as she whispered a sentence. The charm glowed lime green, it felt warm against his chest and then faded. The Elder turned to Damien and repeated the ritual, one by one each received the gift. Then turning to Ronat she offered the final necklace.

'Give this to the mother of Gorlish as a gift, I grant her freedom of Dornachrov.' Ronat bowed, took the charm then whispered something to the Elder who nodded in return. The group were escorted outside while Tom and Damien were asked to take a seat by the fire.

'Let me see your face.' The Elder leant forward and examined Damien's bite marks.

'Ronat said you were bitten by creatures within a cave, is that so?'

'Yes, I couldn't see what they looked like, I think they were after my food.'

'They were Raifien, you were lucky, they usually go for the eyes, a soft and juicy delicacy for Raifien.'

Damien felt the contents of his stomach swirl and churn, his face turned pale at the thought of losing an eye.

'I must treat this at once, then you will both be able to get some rest. Don't worry, it will heal fast.'

The Elder sat Damien on a bench and had him remove his shirt, shuffling away she began to rummage through the shelves and storage jars that filled the eves of the roundhouse. Picking up a jar, shaking her head, sliding it back, she chose another.

'Ah yes.' Fumbling awkwardly she removed the lid. Reaching a withered hand inside she clenched a small amount of its contents and placed this in a wooden bowl. The Elder shuffled along a little more and selected a bunch of dried herbs. The boys gaped intensely at the ritual unfolding before them, intoxicated by the combination of aromas which now filled the room. Stooping over a workbench she began to tear the sprig of herbs and drop them into the bowl.

'Herran!' The young girl they met earlier stepped in from the back room. 'Here, grind these for me.'

Herran picked up the bowl and a pear-shaped stone, pressing down with a circular motion grinding the herbs into powder.

Taking a green bottle, the Elder pulled out the stopper and splashed several glugs of liquid into the bowl to form a paste.

Damien's brow wrinkled and his lips tightened.

'I hope I don't have to drink that.' He whispered.

'Every last drop, and lick the bowl.' Tom responded with a snigger.

Picking up a thin wooden spatula, the Elder approached Damien. Herran held the bowl while the Elder scooped up the paste and began to daub it over each wound.

'Now rest here a while for the poultice to do its work, stay with him Herran, Tom you come with me.'

Tom followed the Elder through a heavy curtain and into the back room of the roundhouse. Unlike the roundhouse, this room was much lighter, a large rectangular room with a wooden staircase to the right. Windows high up in the far wall, oil lamps hanging where the sunlight couldn't reach, and a fire burning in a large open fireplace with two armchairs before it. A writing bureau stood upright against the wall, with bookshelves filling every other wall space available. Beneath the staircase a dark wooden framework housed hundreds of scrolls, each with its own slot and each delicately tied with a thin leather strap. A kitchen table sat proudly in the centre of the room with six wooden chairs around it, the Elder pointed to a chair.

'Please, sit down, I have already asked so much of you, and you have put yourselves at great risk for me already. I am deeply grateful for that,' the elder shuffled over to the fireplace, dipped a hand into her pocket and retrieved her pipe. 'I must ask more of you. We are not safe here, now that the books have regained their power, it has put Dornachrov at risk.' Bending almost double, she took a taper from a jar beside the fireplace and pushed it into the embers, it burst into flame.

'Dornachrov is not as poor a land as it may seem.' She puffed her pipe into plumes of sweet smoke, forming a cloud which spread high across the room.

'We have mines here, mines filled with ember pearl.' Tom, hypnotised by the sweetness of the delicate smoke and gravelled voice of the elder, listened on.

'Ember pearl is a very useful mineral, for many years it was used in jewellery, and it still is, but it has a more powerful side to it.' She coughed and spat into the fire before taking a seat next to Tom. 'It can be used in weaponry, more deadly than a sword or a spear. It brings its own fire and thunder when used with the right skill, and this has become a problem. We kept ember pearl secret for years, but the trade and gifts of old have come back to haunt us. Dornachrov traded with the Yarromites for many happy years, we often paid in ember pearl before we realised its dark secret.' She drew on the pipe again. 'The Yarromites are a devious race, they began to make weapons using ember pearl, they used these to raid other lands, and became almost invincible because of it. Fortunately, ember pearl can only be found in the mines of Dornachrov, unfortunately the Yarromites know this, and they will be coming for it.'

'So now that the books are working again, the Yarromites

will want to come here for more ember pearl?' Asked Tom.

'Correct, and they won't want to trade for it.' The elder sat at the table pointing her pipe towards Tom.

'I need your help again Tom. Dornachrov has few warriors, we are not a fighting race, and we don't yet have the strength to defend ourselves. We need the help of our allies. I must to get a message to the Warriors of Thon, they can be found in a land known as Hagleen.'

'Hagleen, I've seen it in the book, yes, I can do that.'

'Hagleen is a land which is colder and wetter than Dornachrov. There are two kinds of dwellers there, the woodland folk and the town folk. You would be well advised to keep away from the town folk. They can be a ruthless sort, mostly Yarromites left over from the raids. They have taken many to be their slaves and workers over the years. The town itself is more like a fortress, it was once a Yarromite outpost, and the original occupiers were the warriors of Thon, they have now become the woodland folk.'

The Elder's shoulders raised and sank as she paused to take a breath, her eyes fixated on something of nothing, as if to read the past from the smoke rising from her pipe. Pushing herself up from the chair she shuffled over to the scrolls beneath the staircase. Casting a hand over the parchments she gently pulled out one of the faded rolls, untying the leather strap, it slipped to the floor unnoticed. Unrolling the parchment over the table, she pinned its corners with books then studied it carefully.

'This is a map of Hagleen, passed on to me in dreams by Egreth the Elder who dwells there. You will arrive here.' Her withered finger pointed out a spot on the parchment. 'This is a wooded hill with no inhabitants, make your way downhill to this stream.'

A crooked line weaved through the centre of the parchment, Tom couldn't help but notice a large town and castle at one end of it.

'When you reach the stream, you will need to cross it and follow it upstream, downstream will lead you to the city of Hagleen, keep away from there!'

With those last words Tom felt his heart pound and his stomach tighten.

'Follow the river upstream until you reach the standing stone, at this point the stream forks left entering the forest of Thon, follow the stream into the forest until you come to a small wooden bridge,' the Elder traced a skeletal finger to show his path 'cross the bridge and follow the track to the settlement of Thon.' Tapping her finger on the map above a rough sketch of the village.

'Here is where you will find the Chief, give him this.' The Elder pulled a small leather pouch from her pocket and placed it on the table.

'The Chief will direct you from here, and the passing circle to return to Dornachrov is over here.' Again, a withered finger swept across the map, coming to rest on the forest, north of the standing stone.

Tom gazed at the map, the castle and upstream to the standing stone, imagining the journey and how it might look for real.

'I shall ask Ronat to pick some warriors to go with you.'

'No!' snapped Tom 'No, its best if we go alone, we don't want to be noticed, so the less of us the better.'

'Very well then, if you are sure, I am very grateful for the herbs you brought back, in return, take a gift from me.' The Elder shuffled over to an old chest and began to pull items from it.

'Here, help me with these.' She murmured, pulling out a sword and scabbard.

'We don't need these do we?'

'You never know what you might need until you need it.' Croaked the Elder.

'There's a short sword for you, and take this for Damien.'

She pulled out a bow along with a leather quiver filled with arrows. Tom reluctantly accepted the gifts, wondering what on Earth they might need them for.

'You are no longer on Earth Tom.' Chuckled the Elder.

'What, I didn't say anything!'

'No but you thought it.'

'I should have told you; Elders can read thoughts, now go and take a look at your friend, he should be fully recovered by morning.'

Tom picked up the weapons, nodded his thanks to the Elder and returned to find Damien sitting by the fire. The pain had stopped and the swelling eased, but the marks didn't look any better, in fact the poultice made Damien look more like a zombie than anything else.

'Guess I'm the pretty one now!' Laughed Tom.

'Naa, you'll always be ugly.' Replied Damien with a smile.

'The Elder said we can rest here for a while before leaving for Hagleen, oh and she gave me this to give to you.' Tom offered the bow and arrows to Damien.

'What's Hagleen? And why do I get to be Robin Hood? I've never used a bow in my life!'

'I'll tell you later, I have a feeling you won't need to be too good a shot with that so don't worry. Look what she gave me!' Sliding the sword from its scabbard, a razor-sharp blade, lighter than the previous sword and finely engraved with the words "Junett of Esbardach".

'What are we supposed to do with these?' Damian asked, scrutinising the bow.

'You never know what you need to know until you know it.' Tom's face screwed up as he tried to remember the Elder's words.

'What?'

'You never know how ... or was it you never know who? Oh just take it and hope you don't have to use it, I'm knackered let's find somewhere to sleep.'

'I can show you where you can sleep.' A soft voice emanated from the shadows. Herran, stood in the doorway. The darkness of the roundhouse had obscured her golden hair, tied at the back and left to hang down. She wore a long, dark brown skirt, a white blouse tucked in around the waist, tied with a thin belt and purse to one side.

'Oh, thank you!' Replied Damien slightly embarrassed, hastily pulling on his shirt. Neither realised they were not alone.

'This way.' Herran led them through the back room which now stood empty, but for a lingering sweetness of pipe smoke. The staircase whined with footstep-creaks as they climbed up into a large store room filled with sacks and boxes. To the far side of the room a space had been made on the floor where two small wooden beds had been laid out, straw packed down firm and covered with blankets. Extra blankets had been folded and placed on top, and beside each bed lay a tray with a bowl of stew and a mug of liquid.

'Please, make yourself comfortable here, I shall wake you in the morning with breakfast in time for your journey.'

'Thanks, erm, that's very kind of you.' replied Damien. Herran smiled then went back down stairs leaving the boys to eat and rest.

'You fancy her!' Whispered Tom.

'No I don't! I'm just being polite.'

'Yeah right, you being polite! That's got to be the first time that ever happened!' said Tom as the pair of them chuckled quietly then set about devouring the stew.

'Ok, so, what is Hagleen and what's this about a journey?'

'We have another trip tomorrow, it's a long story, but we have to meet some warrior Chief and give him a letter.'

'Cool, delivery boys, that sounds easy. Do you want the rest of that bread?'

Chapter 9
The Cregheligan Book

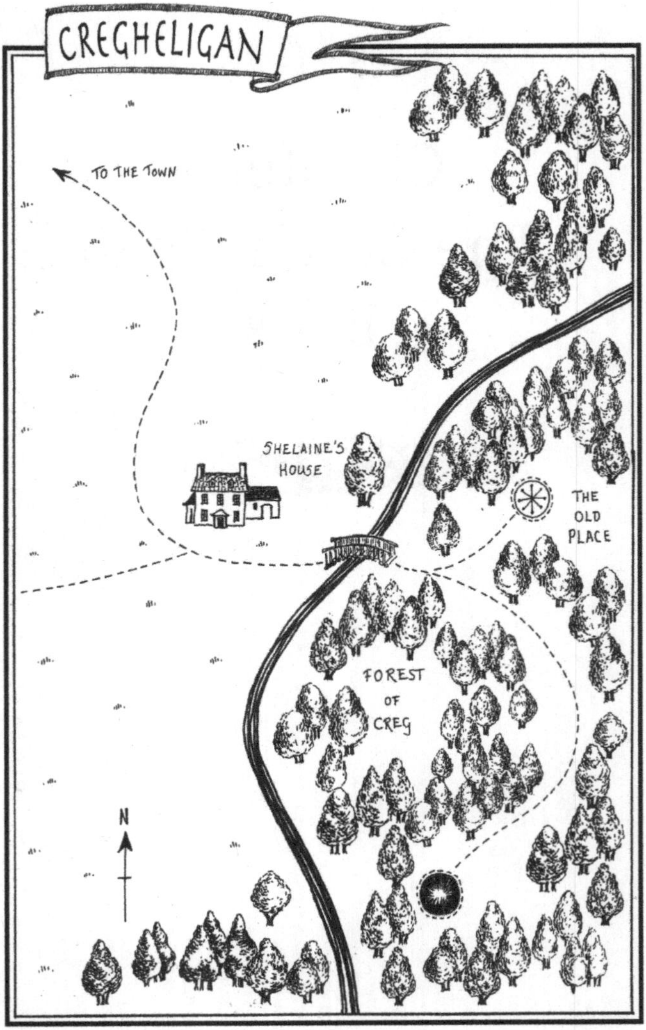
CREGHELIGAN
TO THE TOWN
SHELAINE'S HOUSE
THE OLD PLACE
FOREST OF CREG
N

A humid breeze lifted the rainbow wings of a butterfly across the Meadow Vale. Children, oblivious to its beauty, floated leaf boats down the stream. The silvery water swirled in mercury glossed pools beneath the wooden bridge over which they leaned.

'I win, I win!' shouted Brigaile as her leaf slipped over the waterfall first and into the pool beyond. Juliano and Shelaine laughed and cheered while jostling for second place.

Shelaine's house stood painted golden grey in fading summer evening sunshine. Her father tended to the flowerbeds, neatly pressed up against its cooling masonry. Cregheligan was a beautiful place, kind and gentle folk going about their business with few concerns in life. It was a place of spirituality, peace, open and welcoming to all. There were no cities in Cregheligan, instead, the Creghelt lived in large family homes. Mostly providing for themselves, and meeting in the spiral towered market square to exchange goods and produce.

The towered square was a grand space where the elders would gather, offering wisdom, healing and guidance to those in need. Markets trading in all kinds of goods, from sweet scented baking to delicately embroidered fabrics. Children would play together while parents and grandparents ponder over goods and debate over recent happenings in life. Sipping flower tea beneath the broad emerald leaves of the Derneybray trees, shading their conversations from the heat of the day. A delicate tree which weeps a sweet, honey-like sap from the tips of its leaves. It is said to improve the memory if it were to drip on one's forehead.

'Shelaine! Come now, it's time for dinner.' Hearing this Shelaine looked up from the stream to see father calling from the wooden porch of the house. Shelaine said her goodbyes as she stood claiming second place in the boat race, then ran through the meadow vale towards the distant smell of cooking. The kitchen was that of a country farmhouse, heavy oak cupboard doors and thick roof beams above. A large open fireplace which seemed always to host a welcoming fire, blackened iron pots and pans hugging the chimney breast. Red tiles covered the floor, always cold under bare feet. It felt like more than a kitchen, it was the centre of Shelaine's world, it was the engine which kept the home alive. In the middle of the room was a large rustic dining table, it was enormous. As a young child Shelaine felt it must have existed even before the house, as it couldn't possibly have been brought in afterwards. It was surrounded by heavy dining chairs which groaned against the red tile floor as she dragged one out to perch on.

'Where is mother, isn't eating with us tonight?'

'She will be staying at Tower Square this evening, it's the grand gathering of Elders, but she'll be back tomorrow.'

Shelaine picked up her spoon, sinking it into the large dish of thick stew she thought of how much she would miss her mother's story tonight. Enjoying the hypnotic experience of her mother's warming voice, exploring her way through tattered pages. The deep, slow gruffness of bears, and the twinkling chirping of birds, each playing their part in her tales. Shelaine never could tell if the stories came from the tattered old books, or whether mother made them up as she went along. She was never able to find the passages afterwards, and sometimes the stories changed, but they were always comforting to hear, even though she was fifteen and a little old for them. It was more about the attention her mother gave than the stories themselves.

Shelaine finished her bowl of stew; it left her with a

cosy familiar feeling of comfort inside. She cleared away her place at the table, washed her bowl then left it to dry. Peeping inside the sitting room to find Father curled up with a book in his chair by the fire. She ducked back out and toward the staircase, just like the rest of the house, it was made of dark heavy wood. A thick carpet covered the steps with a little space at either side that Shelaine liked to hop on. From one step to the next, side to side trying not to step on the carpet. The cold touch of each step made her jump faster to the next until she reached the top. Several doors led off from the landing. High above, up in the ceiling was a glass windowed skylight. It let just enough daylight through to make out a tall candlestick which stood in the corner by the top of the stair. Shelaine picked up a match from its box by the candlestick and struck, the tip burst into erratic orange flame as its sulphurous fumes tainted the air. She placed it next to the wick and watched carefully. The waxy cotton slowly took hold of the flame until its radiance out-shone that of the match. Shaking out the match, she dropped it into a small tin on the floor, then turned to face her own tall shadow at the end of the landing. Stepping closer, the tall, slender grey emptiness of the shadow began to reduce from giant to young adult.

Shelaine's room was at the end of the landing next to mother's study. By the time she reached the study door, the tall grey shadow was just that of a teenage girl and no longer menacing. Passing the door to the study she paused, something felt different, more than emptiness. Mother wasn't there tonight, but she felt something else in her absence.

Shelaine took hold of the doorhandle, the cold, brass touch of it made her shiver. Forcing it clockwise until it clicked, she pushed and gently eased inward. A strong comforting aroma of old books and Mother's perfume welcomed Shelaine into the darkness of the room. Twilight broke through the oversized windows at the far end of the study, bathing the contents of the room in gilded warmth. Shards of golden light glanced over the leather topped writing desk, neatly laid out with ink bottles, pens and pale cream paper waiting for its writer. Had there been better light she would have noticed the colours in the carpet beneath her feet, deep burgundy with delicate gold birds stitched into its woollen softness. She was aware of its beauty, as a young child she would crawl across the room giving names to each bird, while Mother sat at her desk studying papers.

To the right, a long bookcase filled the wall from floor to ceiling, thick, dark hardwood shipped from far off lands. Mother would sometimes explain in great detail the journey this bookcase had taken across the seas. For Shelaine, those details were imagined and elaborated on within her mind, she would dream of the bookcase sailing across stormy oceans filled with giant sea monsters, evading pirates and the dangers of the deep.

Tonight, it wasn't the bookcase or the golden birds woven into the carpet which brought her to the study, it was something more than the things she was familiar with. She stared at the bookcase, something felt different, there, a small dusty old book. A book which seemed out of place amongst its companions. Much older, tattier, and the name on the spine together with its contents were unreadable, it stood out for its insignificance, unlike the others. She had seen it many times, it was the only book Shelaine was forbidden from taking out of the study. Maybe it came from the same land as the bookcase, rare and probably quite expensive. Mother would say it was a magic book and not to be played with, Shelaine used to believe this when she was younger and so never touched it, but as she grew older, she formed her own opinions. She drew closer to the shelf, there was a difference about the book, the spine had its usual unreadable text written upon it, but something else caught her attention. Resting a finger on top of the book she eased it out of its place and gently pulled it from the bookcase. Carefully, she opened the cover and saw a map. *Strange, this hadn't been there before,* and she recognised the locations indicated upon it.

From the map she could clearly make out the stream with the bridge where she played today. The forest beyond was recognisable, with a circle marked out a short distance within. The circle appeared to be in what was known as "The Old Passing Place" a stone cobbled area within the forest. Shelaine's house was marked on the map too, and within it, a cross. Shelaine carefully closed the book and quietly made her way out of the study and back downstairs. The light in the kitchen was better and Father would be too busy reading his book to notice. Sitting at the kitchen table she opened the book on the map page again, something wasn't right, something had changed, but she couldn't work out what. Feeling a little bewildered she had an idea. Shelaine crept back upstairs to mother's study, sitting at the desk she opened a slim wooden drawer and took out a pencil and a piece of tracing paper. Opening up the book she carefully placed the paper over the map and marked off the four corners. She then began tracing the outline of the house and some of the details around it, the stream and the bridge, until she had a clear representation of the whole of the map. Shelaine put away the pencil, closed the drawer and went back downstairs to the kitchen table.

She opened the book and carefully aligned the tracing paper with the edges of the map. To her astonishment it didn't align. The map was off centre ever so slightly, but enough for Shelaine to notice what was happening.

Closing the book, she took her shoulder bag from the hook on the door and slipped the book inside. Taking storm lamp from beside the kitchen door Shelaine drew a taper from the jar beside the stove. Lighting it she cupped a hand around the delicate flame and touched the oil-soaked wick, it flickered into life. Closing the glass, she adjusted the height of the wick until the lamp burned bright with a clear flame.

Shelaine picked up the lamp and slung the bag over her shoulder, reaching for the door handle she turned toward the living room, to see Father fully absorbed in his reading.

'I'm just going to take a walk before bedtime Father.'

'Hmm, ok, don't be too long, it'll be dark soon.'

Shelaine opened the door and stepped out into what remained of the daylight. She then realised the lamp wasn't really necessary just yet, but nevertheless, it was a good asset to have and the longer she was out, the more important it would become.

Shelaine set off in the direction of the bridge, the meadow grass was cool against her ankles, the insects had gone to ground and sleepiness was beginning to fall upon the place. For Shelaine this sleepiness went unnoticed, she was fixated upon the prospect of uncovering a mystery. Reaching the bridge, she placed the lamp down on the wooden walkway, carefully opening the book she examined the map. Shelaine felt her heart begin to pound hard as she processed what she saw, the cross was on the bridge, the circle hadn't moved, and the scale of the map had changed. *It's the circle, it wants me to go to the circle.* Hypnotised she snapped the book shut, grabbed the lamp and ran across the bridge. Shelaine had no idea what she would find there, but she knew exactly where it was. Panting and filled with adrenalin she ran down the path to where a small track branched off to the left. It wasn't far, just a few moments away, around her the evening began to close in. The lamp was now serving its purpose, yet at the same time casting shadowy apparitions in all directions. Had she stopped and looked around, she might have felt unsettled at the shapes it cast against the darkened forest, but right now the only thing important to Shelaine was to reach the old place and find an answer to this mystery.

The run slowed to a jog, and the jog slowed to a walk as Shelaine approached the cobblestone clearing. For a moment it felt as though she was stepping onto a stage, an audience of tall Yew trees surrounding her, with the lamp acting as the centrepiece. She walked into the middle of the clearing, large, empty, menacing. Placing the lamp on the ground, she sat cross-legged beside it, then taking a deep breath Shelaine opened the book. The cross lay in the centre of the circle, as the beating of her heart pounded hard against her chest, she turned the next page, it was readable, and the one after, and the one after that.

Sitting still for a few moments she read to herself the title of each page.

Breklon
Elzic
Dornachrov
Devlon
Lowenwrach
Earth
Hagleen
Elmatoch
Yarromovia
Merwag ed Wroth

Shelaine looked around, everything seemed still, quieter than before, she felt isolated, but safe. Then turning to a page at random, Shelaine began to read aloud.

'Elders of the book of Cregheligan,
we seek channel to Hagleen,
through worlds afar,
part the elements,
part time and space,
through the void of existence grant this journey.'

A strange mist began to form, consuming the trees around her, the light from the oil lamp grew dim as it faded away with the trees in the distance. Beneath her, the ground shuddered and vibrated, a strange swirling of light and dark seemed to collide with one another. Then, as the mist began to settle, she found herself no longer in the dark, it was daytime, grey, cold and damp. Tall pine trees surrounded her, stretching high into a grey sky, she looked around, the lamp had disappeared. She wasn't afraid, Shelaine was rarely afraid, she was a strong person whose curiosity took the place of any fear. Besides all this, she could take care of herself, her grandmother had made sure of that. She began to piece together her situation, her surroundings, the sounds and smells that she was now experiencing. The climate was cold and damp, some of the vegetation and even the animal sounds were similar to home, but there were no signs of habitation. She was alone, and that was ok for Shelaine.

Opening the book again she found the pages unreadable, the map was completely different now, with the cross and the circle separate. She studied the map and compared it to her surroundings, after a few moments, she closed the book and started to carefully make her way downhill. There had been a track at some point, but it was very much overgrown now. Huge fallen tree trunks lay around, thick with moss, the route was hard, but not impossible to manage. Shelaine left the main track, finding a log which was just the right height to make a comfortable seat she sat down to check progress. Just as before, the cross had moved and was getting closer to the circle, but she still had some way to go. She wasn't even sure of what she might find at the circle, but she knew there was a better chance of getting home from there. Then she heard something, something behind her, a crackling of branches and scuffling, she stayed motionless, if she moved, she would definitely be spotted, but if she stayed still, she might just be overlooked.

Chapter 10
Hagleen

HAGLEEN
HAGLEEN CASTLE
FOREST OF HAG
RIVER LEEN
FOREST OF THON
N
THON ENCAMPMENT

A cockerel woke Tom at 6:45am, shrill tones piercing the soft sleepiness he'd been enjoying. Cold, fresh morning air filled his lungs causing a faint mist as he breathed out. Tom pulled the blankets tight around his shoulders, slid his legs out of bed and pulled on his jeans fast as he could, the cold denim made him shiver.

'Damien, time to get up mate.' Shaking his friend on the shoulder and receiving a groan of response. Then summoning up all his courage Tom threw back the blankets, quickly pulling on a cold T-shirt, closely followed by a hoodie. He blew into his hands several times until his fingers were capable of tying laces, pulled on his boots and fastened them up.

'Damien come on it's time to get up!' Damien shot Tom a look of hate, then as if he hadn't noticed the cold at all, threw back the covers and began to get dressed. Just as the two of them finished getting ready they heard footsteps on the staircase, Herran appeared.

'Oh, I see you are up already, breakfast will only be a moment, I shall lay it on the table downstairs.'

'Oh, thanks that's very kind of you.' replied Damian nervously. Herran took the trays from the night before and made her way back downstairs.

'Do you realise the last two sentences you said to her were exactly the same! "Oh thanks, that's very kind of you!" provoked Tom, laughing to himself.

'Look I'm going to leave you in Hagleen if you don't pack it in!' Replied Damien, pushing Tom back onto his bed.

The pair tramped downstairs meeting the Elder at the bottom.

'You will find water out the back to wash in, breakfast will be ready when you return.' The boys nodded awkwardly, walking through the back room, which now began to look more like a kitchen. Through a rough wooden door, they stepped into the coolness of the dawn. The sun was awake and shone from a sharp angle across a well-stocked and tended herb garden. Beyond the garden was a wooden frame jutting out from the ground with a rope and water bucket fastened to it. Passing through the garden a sweet and fragrant aroma filled their nostrils with timeless familiarity. It felt cosy, safe and comforting in a strange way. Tom took hold of the bucket and dropped it down into the well, it wasn't very deep, but still created an eerie echo as it hit the water below. There was no pulley, not like in the movies, just a single beam fixed across the top to keep the bucket away from the sides. Tom pulled steadily on the rope until the eerie well gave up its riches, and from it the boys washed as best they could. It seemed to make little difference on the outside, but they did feel fresh and much more awake afterwards.

When they returned to the kitchen, the Elder had gone and two places lay set at the table. Sitting down, they helped themselves to bread, butter and boiled eggs, plenty of it too.

'So, what do you think the "Freedom Of Dornachrov" is?' asked Damien.

'I don't know, maybe it means we can come and go as we please? I'll ask Ronat later, I think he's taking us to the passing circle again.' They continued their meal discussing the previous day's encounter and how next time they might be able to do it better, just as war veterans might. Tom then explained the task they had been asked to complete by the elder, showing Damien the map of Hagleen and how to find the village of Thon.

'How are my warriors this morning then?' enquired Ronat as he entered the room.

'Hi Ronat, we were just talking about you, what does the freedom of Dornachrov mean exactly?' asked Tom.

'Has nobody told you?'

'We never thought to ask.'

'The freedom of Dornachrov is a title, you have both earned the right to own land here in Dornachrov, few folk receive an honour such as this.' Ronat leaned over, taking a chunk of buttered bread. 'I suppose it's because there isn't often a reason to grant it, you should be proud, you have certainly earned it.' He took a bite of the soft bread then poured himself some water. 'When you return from Hagleen I will take you to the lands you have been given.' He mumbled through a mouthful 'We need to be going soon, so I will send out Doon with a party to set up camp by the old fort for when you return. When you're finished here gather your things and we can make a start.' Ronat glugged down the water and went outside.

'We are land owners, that's cool! Do you think it'll come with a house?' Laughed Damien.

The boys replenished their packs with fresh bread and water skins left out by Herran. They checked each other's kit for loose items and then picked up their weapons. When all seemed fine, they left the comfort of the kitchen and stepped outside to meet Ronat in the square.

The sun shone blindingly bright as they walked across the dusty square, people went about their business as usual, smiling and nodding as they passed Tom and Damien, Freemen of Dornachrov. Ronat glanced a wry smile at the boys 'I see you are enjoying your newly found status!'

'I feel like a Lord.' replied Tom, and the three of them laughed as they followed the track in the direction of the forest. As they walked Tom noticed a woman, she stood alone from the rest, she was weeping, quickly wiping tears from her face as she noticed the two boys approach.

'That's the mother of Gorlish.' Said Ronat.

Tom turned and paused; he left the track and walked over to where she stood.

'I'm so sorry, I wish we could have prevented this.'

The woman smiled.

'Gorlish knew what he was volunteering for, you boys did not. Yes, I will miss him, I will miss him every day that I live without him, but he risked his life for a worthy cause. Travel safe and thank you for helping Dornachrov.'

Tom's head hung heavy. *How much suffering have we caused in such short a time?* he tried to push back his thoughts, but couldn't help wondering if they should never have agreed to any of this. He smiled, nodded then returned to the others.

'That was very gracious of you Tom.' Ronat said, leading them out of the village and down through the meadows. 'Death in service of Dornachrov is a thing to be honoured and proud of, Gorlish is now a hero, his name will live on forever in our history.'

The forest was alive with wildlife, scented undergrowth and strange animal sounds heightened their senses with every step. This walk was becoming a little familiar, and with it, the tightness in their stomachs thinking of what might lay ahead. Wilderness surrounded them, strange places, strange people, a constant sense of danger took hold. With every step Tom felt fear, apprehension and excitement all mixed into one sensation. Simply not knowing what was coming next was almost unbearable. Tom tried to lock his thoughts away on the inside, wondering if Damien felt the same, if he did, it didn't show.

They reached the passing circle, the place was just as they left it. Tom took a deep breath before entering the clearing, remembering what happened the last time they passed through this place. Taking the book from his pack,

Damien thanked Ronat once more for showing them the way, then turned to the page which now displayed the title "Hagleen".

'Good luck, and travel safe my friends.' Ronat said turning to walk back to the village. Tom took hold of the book and began to recite the passage.

'Elders of the book of Creghel:gan,
we seek channel to Hagleen,
through worlds afar,
part the elements,
part time and space,
through the void of existence grant this journey.'

The ground shook, vibrating dust and leaves from the floor, a deep tone reverberated throughout the place as everything began to darken around them. Ronat's image slowly faded from view, obscured by a blue foggy mist that swirled about. As the mist began to clear, colours swam around them into shapes, shapes forming into trees as all became still again. The place was quiet and just as the Elder had described. Damp, wet and miserably colder than Dornachrov.

The boys found themselves standing in a natural dip in the ground, deep within a forest on the side of a shallow hill. They stood still for a moment, taking in the new world around them.

'This way, we need to find the river.' Tom led Damien downhill, exactly as instructed. The ground was heavy going, hundreds of years' worth of forest surrounding them on all sides, climbing over fallen trees, upturned roots, avoiding the needling snag of brambles. A slow process as Damien followed carefully behind Tom, his face still a little numb from the poultice.

'This place looks like Scotland, but without the midges,' Damien laughed 'it doesn't look like it's been visited in a long time though.'

'This part probably hasn't, but ... what's that? Over there!' Tom stopped still in his tracks. Both of them went to ground, in the distance Tom had spotted a small figure. 'Look, over there, it looks like a girl, she's reading.'

The boys watched the figure for a moment, she appeared to be alone, then cautiously they made their way towards her. *What if she's from the city, we can't let her leave* thought Tom, his pulse racing with the thought of what they might have to do about her. The girl was sitting on a fallen tree with her back to them.

'Hello, it's ok, there's no need to be afraid' conscious of the weapons they were carrying 'we are just passing through.' Tom said awkwardly 'I'm Tom, and this is Damien.'

'Oh hello, I'm Shelaine, I'm not afraid, I just wasn't expecting anyone else to be around.'

Confident, but also relieved to have at last found company of sorts. Shelaine stood up, and as she did, Tom saw to his surprise the book that she was holding.

'Where did you get that, if you don't mind me asking?'

'This belongs to my mother.'

Damien reached into his bag to retrieve their copy. Tom took the book from Damien and held it up.

'That's exactly the same as mine, where did you get yours?' She asked.

'Well, it's a long story, and we have somewhere to be, but if you'd like to join us we'd be happy to tell you, and show you how to get home, if that's what you were hoping for?' Tom offered. Shelaine smiled and nodded, then the three of them continued through the undergrowth with Tom leading the way. 'We found this book while exploring a wooded hollow back home in England. It was a bit of a surprise when we realised that we could travel with it. You must be from Cregheligan?'

'Cregheligan! Yes, but how did you know that?' Shelaine squinted with an expression of curiosity.

'I guess you don't look like a Yarromite, not that I've ever met one, but they are supposed to be an evil race, so I'm told.'

'Yarromite, I've heard that name before, but I can't recall where.' Replied Shelaine.

'You said the book belongs to your mother? So, I guess she must be the Elder of Cregheligan?'

Shelaine laughed. 'Not the Elder, but one of the Elders, we have hundreds of Elders in Cregheligan.' Shelaine continued 'Something was different about the book this evening, I felt drawn to it, and when I opened it, I could read the map inside, I've never been able to see that before. You say you have somewhere to be, aren't you going home?'

Tom paused for a moment. 'This isn't our first journey, it's actually our third. We left home and travelled to a place called Dornachrov, there we met the Elder, she then asked us to go to Magellion to gather flowers, and now we are on our way to find help from the Warriors of Thon.'

'To pick more flowers? They must really like flowers in Dornachrov.' Shelaine smiled with a look of mischief.

'No not for flowers, for warriors to defend against the Yarromites when they invade.'

'This is all very confusing, so how come you are involved in all of this? Couldn't you just go home, and why would the Yarromites invade?'

'I guess we were the cause of it. You see, when we found the book, it brought two more books back to life. Now all three books are working, you have one, we have one, and the Yarromites have the other.' Tom Led the way down hill, Shelaine behind him trying to piece together the story. 'These books were created by your people to spread peace, which was very noble of you. But, the Yarromites stole one and began to raid other lands with it, that's why the Creghelt sent this book away to be lost, so that all three would lose their power.'

Trudging on behind, Damien absorbed the conversation, it wasn't that he didn't care, he was more focused on what was to come from this place. The environment here looked less welcoming than Dornachrov, he felt someone should at least be keeping an eye out.

'But why can't you just go home and send the book away again, wouldn't that stop the Yarromites?' Shelaine asked.

'Well, according to the Elder in Dornachrov, the book can only be sent away by the Elders of Cregheligan. We haven't got around to doing that yet, and it will take a little planning. You see, we don't want to end up stuck in a strange land.'

Shelaine nodded and turned her eyes back to the path ahead. In the distance, the sound of flowing water bubbled and echoed through the trees, and with it, a familiar damp, earthy scent of vegetation. Approaching the shallow stream, they began to look for a way to cross. To the North, beyond the stream, the forest opened up onto a vast green landscape. In the distance, they could make out the three grey towers of Hagleen Castle, stretching high up above the city. A haze of woodsmoke hovered about the castle. Around the castle wall slumped ramshackle houses and places of work, a faint outline of what was once a ditch surrounded the whole of the city. This formidable stronghold appeared to burst at the seams with over popularity, and the further out from the city, the poorer the place looked. In the fields around Hagleen could be seen farmers and farmhands going about their work. Oxen pulled ploughs and carts, riders on horseback ambled about the fringes as if to guard against wolves or prevent escapees, it was hard to tell. The trio were safe enough, much distance lay between them and the farmland, but all the same, they chose to remain low in the shadows of the pine forest.

The stream wasn't particularly wide, but quite fast flowing, as Tom led them North in search of the bridge. The going under foot was much easier now, fewer trees and bushes hindered their way, but it also made for less cover should they need it. Damien kept a watchful eye, if the horsemen appeared now, they were all at risk of being captured. They continued at a more hurried pace, keeping lookout as best they could until finally it came into view. Farther upstream in the distance, a standing stone, just as the Elder had described, right beside it a bridge. The stone stood tall and slender with unrecognisable markings on all four sides, its top had been shaped to a point, and beneath it, the stream forked. Tom led them over the bridge as instructed, took the left fork and into the shadows of the Forest of Thon.

The treeline stood lower than that of Dornachrov, yet the density was thicker. Wildlife was in abundance, it sounded very similar to back home, rooks, pheasants and a solitary cuckoo could all be heard within the depths of the forest. These familiar sounds were comforting, but they didn't make the journey feel any less daunting.

Tom led the way up through the wood, tree roots and dense thicket made the going tougher than before, and there was no obvious path. Tom drew his sword and took a swing, after several blows, he managed to open up a route and the three of them squeezed through the natural barricade of thorny growth. This section of the stream was little more than a few paces wide, but fast flowing nevertheless, they followed it deeper into the forest. Tom clearing the way whenever needed, and as the protection of the forest allowed them to slow their pace, the adrenaline began to subside.

Pre-occupied with the undergrowth, they almost missed the bridge. It was old and moss covered, a few rotting posts pushing up from the stream bed to support it, while the track beyond lay overgrown and barely visible. Crossing the stream they followed the overgrown path deeper into the forest.

'This doesn't seem right, it's too overgrown, there's supposed to be a settlement at the end of this path.' Tom, still leading the way, was beginning to have doubts.

'There doesn't seem to be much sign of life around here. Do you think the Elder could have got it wrong, maybe the town folk captured them?' Replied Damien.

They continued on regardless and soon the path opened up into a clearing, a group of small huts evenly spaced around the edges. Animal pens and storage shelters for food and firewood, but the place was completely deserted. It was worse than deserted, it was derelict.

'Well, I guess that's it then, there's nobody left.' Tom shrugged, dropping his rucksack to the floor beside the ruins of a wall.

From its appearance the settlement had been uninhabited for a long time, roofs had fallen in and undergrowth grew tall across paths and inside the simple dwellings.

'I wasn't expecting this, what do we do now?' Asked Tom.

'I don't suppose we have much choice, let's grab some lunch.' answered Damien, looking for a place to sit.

Shelaine began to look around for any sign of recent

habitation. The houses were of simple construction and empty within, nothing remained of their previous occupiers, and each house was the same.

'Look, over there, the path continues on' Shelaine pointed to the far side of the settlement. 'maybe we haven't reached it yet?'

'Well spotted! Here, try some of this, it's delicious.' Replied Tom.

The boys shared out their sweet bread and water. Once fed and watered they were beginning to feel the cold and damp, they began packing away their remaining supplies and prepared to move off again. Shelaine looked on as the boys double checked each other's packs, smiling at the routine of the two young warriors.

'Where did you two learn your field craft skills?'

'We are mostly self-taught, but our school library has a couple of good survival books.' Replied Damien.

Shelaine grinned. 'Good knowledge to have.'

'Open the book and let's see the map' asked Tom, the pair tried to work out where they were in comparison to the standing stone, as it was the obvious marker point to work from. Resting the book on a fallen tree, Tom traced a finger from the stone to the settlement when a heavy thud struck the tree in front of him. He jumped back to see an arrow sticking out from the log as another slammed in next to it.

'Lay down your arms!' A voice called out from the forest, the trio looked around, but saw nothing then another arrow struck the log just a few centimetres from the other two, the boys dropped their weapons raising their hands in disbelief. Three men rushed out of the undergrowth from behind and surrounded them.

'We have a message for Eskin Chief of Thon.' shouted Tom as he was forced to kneel, his head pushed down over the log.

'No, please no, we came from Dornachrov with the Book.' cried Damien, as he and Shelaine were dragged over to the same log and forced to kneel next to Tom, each gasping for breath. Necks forced hard against the trunk by the leather boots of two warriors, hands twisted across their back. A sword came up under Tom's chin, as tears and sweat dripped from his face running down the polished blade.

Chapter 11
The Warriors of Thon

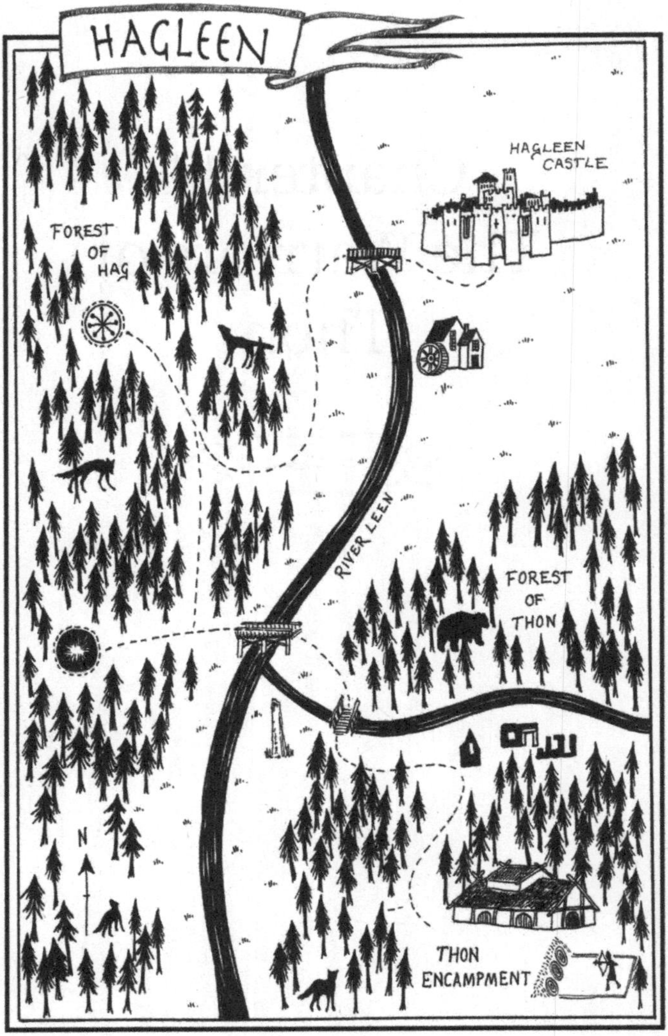
HAGLEEN
HAGLEEN CASTLE
FOREST OF HAG
RIVER LEEN
FOREST OF THON
N
THON ENCAMPMENT

Tom felt the razor-sharp edge of the sword pressed up against his throat. He held as steady as he could, avoiding any movement which might cause the blade to slice into his skin. Then the weight was released from his back and a hand dragged him by the hair to his knees. In front of him stood a large man dressed in animal skins, holding a huge sword in one hand, and the book in the other.

'Is this yours?' growled the man. Tom rubbed his throat and tried to speak; his mouth was dry as he trembled out the words.

'Yes, we travelled from Dornachrov with it, we have a message from the Elder for the Chief of Thon.' The man stared at Tom then carefully examined the book, turning to the warrior holding him, he motioned his head to lift Tom to his feet.

'I know of Dornachrov, and of this book, what's this message you speak of?'

'In my pack.' Replied Tom.

The warrior took Tom's pack and shook out its contents. Picking up the leather pouch he glanced suspiciously at Tom and opened it. Sliding out the letter he unfolded it and read the message. At the same he motioned to his warriors to release the other two, seeing this gesture Shelaine shook off her captors and stood upright.

The warrior folded the letter then placed it back in the pouch, examining both boys around the neck he clipped Tom around the back of the head.

'Ah you'll be alright, but if you're going to carry a weapon, respect it and learn how to use it.' He barked at the pair, then turned to Shelaine. 'I hope we didn't frighten you too much young lady.' Shelaine said nothing, her face remained expressionless other than a slight indication of a grin. He laughed and turning to Damien handed them back the book.

'Pick up your things, I suppose the least I can do is feed you, my name is Eskin and I'm the Chief of Thon.' His tone turned friendly as the guards patted their respective captives on the back, laughing as they handed back their weapons. 'Come on, let's get you to the village.'

One warrior led the way and one took the rear, the Chief walked in the middle and began to tell his story.

'We were raided several years ago; we had to abandon the old settlement. The horsemen are much stronger these days, taking risks they once never dared to. We are forced mount guards and patrols constantly to avoid raids, if we hit them first, they retreat fairly quickly and with a few less horsemen.' Eskin laughed and his warriors joined in.

'They don't like the taste of Edrik's arrows!' replied one.

'Nor Hedoth's spear!' Laughed the other.

'The truth is, Hagleen Castle is much stronger than it was, and we have lost several men to its raids recently, including my own son, Ackron. They hold him captive as we speak.'

The three newcomers listened on while they walked for an hour or so, as the Chief described their current situation. Eskin led the group off the track and into a thicker part of the forest. The smell of cooking from the new settlement began to fill the damp air, mixing with woodsmoke as they made their way to the top of a ridge. Two heavily built warriors dressed in animal skins stood guard, each held a spear in hand. Both the men had a bow slung over their backs and a short sword hung from their belts. Beyond the guards a track continued over the ridge and down into a wide and shallow valley, several dozen huts lined out along it. This was a large and well defended settlement, built in an area which offered good natural defences.

The two guards acknowledged their Chief and the warriors as they passed through the settlement. The huts were basic, round houses made of wattle and daub with roofs thatched using anything that might keep out the rain. Some were simple shelters built up against craggy outcrops of stone, one thing they all had in common was a fire. A mother nursed her baby besides the doorway to one of the huts, while chickens roamed around. The carcass of a deer hung from a pole between two huts, alongside it two deer hides stretched tight across wooden frames. Smoke bellowed out from the top of some huts, while others had firepits set out in front with large iron tripod frames built above for holding pots. Farther up the track stood a large wooden hall, inside, a group folk huddled around a fire. This was a poor community, constantly hindered by raids, Tom looked on in sadness at what he saw, feeling the need to help in whatever way he could.

They approached a large hut with two guards positioned outside. Eskin's hut, a fire burned bright in the centre with chairs, benches and tables set about. Beyond the fire a thick rug covered the floor, in the centre stood an ornately carved wooden throne where Eskin heaved himself down. The three of them sat by the fire on a bench, Eskin's wife brought them each a cup of hot liquid that smelt of honey.

'There, that should warm you up.' Damien smiled glancing at Tom, then took a sip. It certainly did, it was mead.

The Chief sat facing the three of them. 'So, Dornachrov needs warriors, the last time this request was made, our ancestors didn't respond, and as a result we lost Hagleen Castle.'

'Hagleen castle was yours?' Enquired Shelaine.

'Hagleen castle is ours! It was taken from us by the

Yarromites when they stormed through Dornachrov and into Hagleen.' Eskin's wife handed him a large goblet of mead. 'We warriors were not as strong back then, and when the Creghelt sent away one of their books to stop the Yarromites, several hundred of them were stranded here.' The Chief took a sip of the hot brew and continued. 'They over-ran the castle and gradually strengthened their hold, applied their policies, charged their taxes and executed those who got in their way. We will not allow the Yarromites into this land again, so we will defend Dornachrov.' Running his fingers through his beard the Chief paused. 'There is, however, an obstacle in our way. The city folk hold my son Ackron in that castle, and I want him back. He's the only one that can help Dornachrov, I'm too old for battle now.' Raising his mug to his bearded lips he took a long slurping drink from it, then pointed to Damien. 'You have a bow there, where did you get that?'

'The Elder of Dornachrov gave me this, but I've never used it.' Replied Damien.

'Well, that bow is nothing special, but those arrows are. It would be wrong of me to ask to borrow your weapons, but if you're coming to Hagleen Castle with us, you'll need to know how to use them.'

Tom glanced up from his drink. 'Coming to Hagleen Castle with you?'

'Yes, we need to get my son back so that he can lead his men in the battle for Dornachrov. You will need some practice if you're going to fight the Yarromites, and neither of you look like you've seen much combat. Besides, it's those arrows I'm interested in, finish your drinks and I'll show you what I'm talking about. The girl can help wash the mugs.' As he heaved himself from his chair.

Shelaine jumped to her feet. 'I'm not your slave! I shall fight too, and I don't need a fancy bow.' Shelaine shot a hand behind her back and threw something at speed causing a dull thud from the back of the hut. The Chief stumbled back into his chair with a huff and looked around, in the centre of a narrow post was embedded a slender throwing knife.

Tom jumped to his feet in shock 'What the f, Shelaine!'

The Chief let out a roaring laugh 'You're not a Dornach!' He bellowed out.

'I'm Shelaine, daughter of Henwen, Elder of Cregheligan.'

Still laughing the Chief turned to his warriors. 'Then how can we fail boys! You can teach us all how to fight, Shelaine, daughter of Henwen, Elder of Cregheligan!'

The laughter continued, but not in mockery, in confidence, as the Chief led them out of the hut.

'Edrik! Fetch arrows and a couple of bows. Today we train, tomorrow we fight!' He roared.

The Chief led them through the encampment into a much larger area, where long huts lined the path. These were barracks, accommodation huts for warriors, and plenty of them. Warriors of heavy build, draped in animal skins sitting by camp fires, some sharpening knives or swords, while others prepared and inspected arrows, getting ready for battle.

'It's just like medieval times, our history teacher would love this!' Tom said, looking around in awe.

'Vikings! These are real Vikings.' Muttered Damien.

'Ok, I get it, you're obsessed with Vikings, but I'll hand it to you, these do look like proper Vikings.' Said Tom, wondering what was coming next.

The Chief took them to a clearing, a line of straw filled sacks hung from wooden frames at the far end. A mound of earth surrounded the whole area creating a barrier. Just in front of the party a row of logs had been pegged into the ground with wooden stakes forming a firing point.

'Edrik, bow.' Shouted the Chief.

Edrik handed a bow and quiver of arrows to the Chief. Placing an arrow on the bowstring the Chief drew back and released. The arrow struck hard into its target, dead centre. The Chief then handed an arrow to Damien.

'Try with this one first.'

Damien took the bow from his shoulder and clumsily fumbled with the arrow, he dropped it and picked it up again.

'Here, let me show you, copy me.' Edrik stood beside Damien and holding his own bow, placed an arrow on the bowstring and drew back, Damien copied him, drew back and released. Damien's arrow went low and hit the ground, while Edrik's arrow struck the target beside the Chief's.

'Hold the bow steady and draw back again.' Edrik advised.

Damien repeated the process, each arrow he loosed getting slightly closer to its mark.

The Chief looked on with a grin. 'I think that's close enough, now try one of your own arrows, but aim a little higher this time.'

Edrik smiled and stepped back as Damien slipped one from his quiver. It was furnished with red flight feathers and wrapped with finely woven cloth close to the arrow head, slightly heavier and thicker than the previous arrows. Placing it on the bowstring he slowly drew back then released. The red feathered arrow whirled from the bow and down the range, as its tip struck slightly low on target a bright orange flash erupted with a thunderous roar. The target exploded, blasting splinters of wood and clouds of straw high up into the air. The smoke swirled around as pieces of wood and clumps of debris landed all about them. The Chief and his warriors collapsed in fits of laughter, while Damien's face glowed with excitement. 'Bloody hell! The Elder never mentioned that!'

Tom looked on in horror, 'So I've been escorting a walking bomb for the past day? That's all I need, an idiot like you, with a bag full of explosives.'

Shelaine said nothing, just beamed a smile while plucking fragments of straw from her hair.

'Edrik, find the three of them some accommodation, get them fed and rested. Then tell them our plans for tonight. Oh, and you might want to keep those away from the fire!' Laughed the Chief, pointing to Damien's arrow quiver.

'Yes Chief!' Replied Edrik, still laughing at the explosion.

The chief turned to another warrior 'Hedoth!'

'Chief!'

'Could you organise a work party to rebuild the archery range.'

'Yes Chief.' Hedoth laughed turning to make his way through the fallen debris and back towards the barracks.'

Edrik escorted the three of them to a small barrack block close to the archery range.

'We use this as a shelter when the range is busy, but it's empty right now.' Hedoth pushed open the wooden door, it was basic, furnished with wooden beds and benches around the sides, with a large fire pit in the middle of the room. 'I'll have some food and blankets brought over, you can stay here until tonight. Get some rest, we are leaving for Hagleen at dusk, I'll come and collect you when it's time.'

It was noon, with a good few hours of daylight left, but they were tired and the excitement of the day was beginning to take a toll on them. Soon after Eskin had left there was a knock at the door, an old man and woman dropped off a large pot of soup, some bread, a jug of warm mead and blankets for them.

'At this rate we're going to be wasted by dusk.' Laughed Damien as he ladled out soup into three wooden bowls.

'Where did you say you come from?' Asked Shelaine, as she poured out the mead.

'Hinckleford, England, Earth' Replied Tom, 'I don't think I've pronounced it that way before, but that's where we're from.' Tom smiled.

'I've never heard of it, but I'm guessing it must be quite primitive if you can't use a bow?'

'Hmm, yes, it's primitive in Hinckleford alright. We can't even get a decent broadband connection.' Tom laughed.

As Tom and Shelaine chatted, Damien began to build a fire in the pit. Taking some small sticks and four logs from a pile in the corner, he placed two flat and two more on top to cross them. With a handful of straw, he packed the inner and then added smaller sticks on top, finally taking a box of matches from his pack, he lit the straw at the bottom, it instantly burst into flames and began to catch light to the sticks. He was a self-taught expert at fire lighting, and loved it. Tom had often referred to him as a pyromaniac, a name which Damien seemed to relish in.

The conversation began to slow as the warmth of the fire and mead took hold. By now, each had pulled a straw bed closer to the middle of the room, forming a triangle around the fire pit. Boots close to the fire and jackets hanging up at the side to dry, they drifted off to sleep in the fragrant wood smoke, to the sound of crackling logs.

Chapter 12
Hagleen Castle

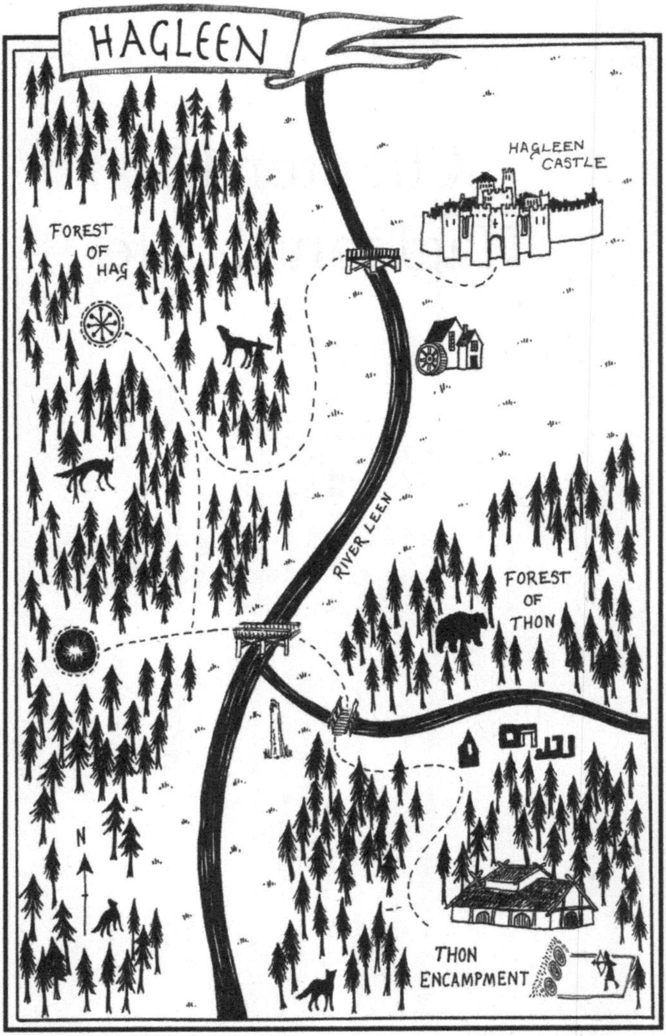
HAGLEEN
HAGLEEN CASTLE
FOREST OF HAG
RIVER LEEN
FOREST OF THON
N
THON ENCAMPMENT

The warmth and cosiness were shattered as Edrik swung open the door. Wind and rain howled in after him before he could slam it shut again.

'Here, you're going to need these.' Placing some water skins and baked bread rolls on the table. The fire had burned down to a comforting pile of glowing embers, excited into flame again by the opening of the door.

Shelaine slipped on her boots now warmed by the fire, stood, and walked over to the table.

'Are you boys getting up, or should I pour water over you?' She mocked, holding up a water skin.

Edrik laughed. 'Make your way to the Chief's hut once you're packed, we'll be leaving shortly.' Ducking out of the doorway the wind and rain excited the embers of the fire again as he slammed the door shut after him.

The boys were sitting up now, pulling on boots in zombie-like fashion. Shelaine inspected the provisions brought in by Edrik, before packing a share into her bag beside her book. She reached behind her back, easing the small throwing knife from its scabbard. The knife had a slim, gold handle, wrapped with silver thread and a shiny silver blade. It was given to her by her grandmother, who was once a warrior many years ago. Shelaine's own mother chose to be an Elder, but Shelaine had always wanted to follow in the footsteps of her grandmother, and so learned how to use the knife. Secretly practicing every day in the forest, almost every tree felt the sting of its blade. This was meant to be, her grandmother had prepared her for it, and it felt good. Shelaine enjoyed playing with the others, racing leaf boats down the stream and lazy summer days, but she also loved the excitement, freedom and danger this book offered her.

Tom and Damien both packed the extra provisions into their rucksacks, once again checking everything was secure and didn't rattle. This was important, now more than ever, a slight rattle coming from a backpack could alert someone, and this time there was more at stake than a ripped trouser leg from a farmer's dog.

Outside, the wind had picked up, blustering rain across a fading grey sky as dusk crept in. Campfires blazed by the wind, firefly sparks darted about as they walked back towards the Chief's hut. Dark silhouettes moving about the place with urgency, a noticeable sense that something dangerous was about to take place. As they re-joined the main track a group of warriors could be seen in the distance outside of the Chief's hut.

'Over here!' Edrik spotted them approaching.

'You have all your things?'

'Yes, all packed.' Replied Tom.

The Chief ducked out of his hut and the group went silent.

'Inside, gather round the fire.'

The furniture had been moved to the sides of the hut, in the centre, a rectangle had been formed with four thin poles, the ground flattened smooth within. The Chief sat on a stool and leaned forward. Smoothing out the earth in front of him, he took a stick from the fire's edge and began marking out a plan of the castle on the ground.

'Follow the river down to the mill.' Pointing to the waterwheel scratched into the earth. 'From here you leave the river and make your way to the tannery.' Drawing a line through the town. 'There is a way into the castle, but not big enough for an army. Some of you will remember using it on raids to steal food in the winter.' On the ground he scratched a mark over the castle wall. 'Here you will find a tanner's workshop built against the outer wall, at the back of the workshop there are some empty barrels, behind these is a small hole in the wall big enough to crawl through. On the other side of the wall is the castle grain store, from there you will need to find your own way.'

The group consisted of Edrik as leader, Hedoth, his second in command, and three other warriors all just as mighty in appearance. Tom, Damien and Shelaine would also accompany them.

'You are probably curious as to why I'm sending these three along with you.' The Chief pointed with his stick to the trio.

'These two carry weapons of Dornachrov, and this one is a weapon in herself, she's Creghelt.' The three warriors looked on in astonishment, and grinned.

'Use their skills and bring them back safe, something just as important awaits after this.'

Edrik acknowledged, took one last look at the plan, which he was already familiar with from a previous winter raid, and then led the troop off into the blackness beyond the warmth of the camp fires.

The twilight seemed darker after leaving the camp, the glow from torches and campfires had destroyed what night vision they had, this was expected and it would take time to regain. Each kept close in single file, silent, with just the dull, methodical trudge of footsteps against the wind and rain. The path was a vague pale greyness, ever so slightly lighter than the vacuous blackness of the forest. It would have been difficult to navigate the thickly woven brambles and fallen trunks by daylight, but at night, it was almost impossible. The chatter and screeching of nocturnal creatures stirred in all directions, echoing through the invisible undergrowth. Tom gripped tight on the hilt of his sword, it felt reassuring that there was something there to protect him. At that exact moment it occurred to him that he had never used it against an enemy. It was too late to think about that now, he felt stupid for not properly training with the sword, learning how to swing and fight with it, but nevertheless, he held it tight. The track continued on through the old village, towards the sound of distant splashing water, water which would lead them to Hagleen Castle.

Footsteps changed tone passing over the wooden footbridge, continuing along stream to the edge of the forest where it joined the river. By now they had regained full night vision and could make out silhouettes in the distance, tree trunks stood ghostlike, watching these passers-by. This felt even more eerie than not seeing them at all, confusing movement with the mischief of darkness playing its tricks.

The forest edge began to creep into view, and with it the troop went to ground. In the distance, Hagleen Castle stood formidable, orange flames from far off torches flickered around the battlements and towers like tiny sparks. From this distance the place looked impregnable and well defended.

'Take a few moments, have some water, it's going to get a little riskier from here.' Edrik said.

They sat in darkness and silence, huddled at edge of the forest they sipped from water skins. The rain had stopped, but the wind brushed through, playing with the branches above. On Edrik's word, like thieves they scrambled out of the tree line, through the grassy meadow and dropped down onto the pebble bank of the river. The bed of the river was wide, resembling a cobbled road snaking its way gracefully towards the town. Stumbling slowly and clumsily along; it wasn't the easiest of routes to follow and hard to get a precise idea of where they were in relation to the castle. This didn't matter, they knew they had to leave the safety of the riverbed upon reaching the mill.

Gradually the air began to change, the smell of sewerage

and animals caught the breeze, filling nostrils with its sour stench. The distant bark of a dog went some way toward helping them identify their location. Edrik halted the party then edged his way cautiously up the riverbank. Squinting and slowly scanning the horizon, three towers loomed over the tall, grassy verge. Two figures on one of the walls walked slowly toward the gatehouse, silhouetted by torchlight from the Keep behind. Edrik could just make out the top of a waterwheel in the misty greyness adjoining a mill further downstream. This would be the most dangerous point of their mission so far, leaving the shelter of the riverbed and heading for the tanner's workshop. At the base of the castle wall stood workshops and houses crammed together, making use of every space they could. The walls offered strong support and shelter from the wind, and from this angle the castle appeared impossible to breach. Edrik slid back down the bank to where the others were waiting.

'The mill is just a few hundred paces downstream; I can see the wheel from the top of the bank. It won't take us long to get there, so this is probably the last chance we'll get to focus on what lies before us.' Edrik paused 'Hagleen Castle is our home, we should be the ones living, working and sleeping there now. This is the first step to regaining that home.'

Tom felt a pang of emotion strike home hearing those words *these people need their home back* he thought. The warriors nodded in resolute agreement as Edrik turned, leading them slowly downstream in the direction of the mill. The river started to narrow and gradually became deeper; the far side of the riverbank steepened to a sharp incline. Following the bending river, snaking their way downstream, the sounds and smells became louder and stronger above the rushing, babbling water. Looming before them, as they turned a bend in the river, the skeletal silhouette of a waterwheel came into view.

A wooden structure, built to channel water from the river to the wheel branched off ahead of them. The wheel slowly turned clockwise with the force of water pouring onto it. A stone, thatched cottage supported the wheel, while alongside it propped a small animal shed. The sound of the river was loud against the stillness of the night as the group crept up the bank to peer over.

Lying flat near the top of the riverbank; the cover of long grass helped ease any nerves. Before them, the castle walls towered above, they were too close now to see the Keep and the torches of the guards beyond. A faint amber glow flickered from the walls in several places, but no other movement could be seen. At the base of the Castle wall stood the outer buildings, shops and workshops lacking any planning or order, and between them, a confusing pattern of alleyways.

'Follow me.' Edrik lunged from cover, running crouched toward a small barn. One by one the group followed with Hedoth at the rear. Reaching the barn, they knelt in the shadow and listened, nothing, no sound of movement or alarm. Peering around the barn Edrik checked that the alley beyond was clear, then set off again.

The fear and excitement were really starting to kick in now, Tom could feel his heart beating faster and deeper. The stench of the place was strong; alleyways covered with rotting waste and animal dung. Beyond the warriors in front of him, Tom could see the Castle wall and the buildings that leant against it, just another two alleys to cross. They crouched and ran to the next building, a blacksmiths workshop, open on two sides with a fire still hot from the days' work before. Sheltering inside, Edrik scanned the workshops at the base of the castle wall, the

Tanners workshop was large and easy to find, animal skins of all kinds pinned to frameworks against the walls, rabbit, deer and bearskins. The building stood proud, one of few with an upper floor. A double doorway to the front of the building had been left slightly ajar, and it was towards this that Edrik led the group.

This final alleyway was dark and close to the castle wall, making the last leg of their journey easier, there was less chance of being seen. Edrik disappeared through the tanner's doorway, the place stank, even worse than outside, one at a time they slipped through behind him, then waited for their eyes to adjust to the blackness within.

Creeping forward towards the far wall they could just make out a stack of small barrels, slowly, and silently they started to move them to form a fresh pile in front. The barrels were empty making it an easy a job, but still they had to work quietly. Soon the whole stack had been re-positioned a meter or so away from the wall, revealing a small hole large enough to crawl through. Edrik crawled in first, followed by the others, slowly and methodically moving in synchronicity. It was black dark and damp, the invaders shuffled along the tunnel, passing through the giant castle wall on hands and knees. The sound of what might have been rats in front of them sent a shiver down Damien's spine as he recalled flashbacks from the cave back in Magellion. Then gradually, a faint glow could be seen up ahead as one by one the warriors pushed through and over the top of a grain pile. Each of them sank knee deep into the grain as they emerged from the tunnel, they were inside.

The light was better here, but only just, Edrik crept over to the barn door at the far side, it was locked. A warm amber glow shone from the torches hanging on the inner castle walls. At various points the light broke through cracks in the door, causing the grain to glow like a mountain of gold. Laughter and talking could be heard coming from a small tavern on the far side of the castle courtyard, other than that, nothing else stirred. Edrik studied the surroundings through a crack in the door, the keep looked formidable, a huge stone structure with a solid door at the front, no window openings below the second floor. To the right of the keep was a large wooden building built alongside it, at its highest point the roof of that building came almost level with a second-floor window.

By now Hedoth had joined Edrik, both peering through the gap in the door.

'If we follow the wall around, we could climb up onto that roof at its lowest point, then get into the Keep through the window.' Edrik shared his plan with Hedoth as Tom and Damien listened on. 'The roof of the building is shaded by the Keep it should offer good cover too.' Hedoth nodded in agreement, feeling sure they could climb onto the sloping roof.

As the two warriors discussed the route, Shelaine was examining the lock on the door. Taking a slender metal object from her pocket, she carefully inserted it into the lock, gently rotating and twisting it in the keyhole, the lock eased open with a muffled click.

'Nice work my girl, the Chief was right about you.' Whispered one of the warriors.

'I'd rather you call me by my name, Shelaine.' As she folded and slipped the fine tool back into her pocket, grinning smugly. Edrik nodded in appreciation and carefully pulled the door inwards; it creaked slightly as they listened for any sign of disturbance. There was no indication they had aroused suspicion, and so they filed through the open doorway.

The party moved quickly along the inner wall buildings, hugging the shadows as best they could, still no guards could be seen, they were higher up on the walls above, and certainly not expecting intruders. The ground was soft and silent to tread, straw-covered mud cushioned their footsteps as they padded along.

Ahead of them stood a monstrous round tower with a stone staircase leading up to a closed wooden door. A burned-out torch hung from the side of the staircase allowing them to pass by unnoticed in the shadows. Circling the tower they proceeded along the north wall. In front of them stood the wooden building pressed up against the side of the keep. Edrik turned to two of his warriors. 'Keep guard here in the shadows of the building.' The two of them nodded and went to ground.

The roof was high against the keep, sloping gently down to a more manageable height where the eight of them now crouched. Two warriors lent their backs against the wooden store, bent their knees and cupped their hands to form foot holds. Edrik went first, heaved up onto the roof followed by Hedoth. Waiting in the shadow of the Keep, they watched as the rest of the group were slowly raised to join them. On all fours, one by one they moved towards the window. The roof crackled as they crawled, straw scratching at palms padding forward like cats. Tom, third in line looked up to see Edrik silently disappearing into the deep blackness of the window, Hedoth followed, then it was Tom's turn, quickly pulling himself up and into the unknown. Eyes once again became useless at this point, there was nothing but blindness before him and the pale grey rectangle of the window behind, now filled with the silhouette of Damien, closely followed by Shelaine.

Each second ticked away slower than the one before, the fear of being found combined with the desire to push himself deeper into a darkened corner for safety, fear pulled hard at him. A final shadow now began to ease itself through the window and then gently settle down beneath it. The third warrior would stay by the window in order to raise the alarm should the others below get into trouble. Edrik took hold of Hedoth's arm and gently tugged, this was the signal to repeat on down the line and begin to move off. Edrik, whose eyes had now adjusted ever so slightly, could make out a door, they were in what appeared to be a small clerical room. He lifted the latch slowly and carefully pulled at the solid oak door; a feint glow could be seen in the distance. Edrik led them out of the room into a much larger hall, several rows of equally spaced tall clerical desks filled the room, and to the right stood another heavy door which was closed. The party slipped their way past the closed door and along the wall to where the feint glow could be seen. They reached the entrance to a spiral staircase leading both up and down, cautiously grasping sword scabbards and anything else that might clatter against the stone steps, they made their way down. The place had a strong aroma of beeswax and old library books. The flame of a burning oil lamp added to that aroma, its dim glow guiding them to the stair. The Keep was silent as they continued on down the staircase, Edrik knew that if Ackron was still alive he would be held in the dungeon, what he didn't know was how well he might be guarded.

The group slowly coiled their way down the stairwell. Sweeping clouds offered sporadic flashes of moonlight through arrow slits as they descended. Edrik paused as they approached the ground floor, it was the great hall, leading to the main entrance of the keep. A cavernous hall steeped in darkness, the only light coming from the orange flame of a torch hooked to the wall by the stairwell. Fear and excitement mixed together to create what felt like a third sense, an awareness of what was beyond sight and sound, Tom had never felt more alive. The strong smell of beeswax began to fade to a mix of leather and sweat as they descended to the next level, the smell of warriors. Snoring could be heard ever so softly in the distance, death had never felt so close. On passing this floor there was no torch to offer a glimpse of what lay beyond the darkness, just a feint glow from above and the same from below. The temperature began to drop, the smell of leather and sweat now mixed with damp and filth. Other noises, smaller noises, scuffling and scratching, distant noises, obscured by the monotony of the seemingly never-ending steps.

A single torch burned dimly against the wall, complimented by the glowing embers from an iron brazier in the centre of the room. The floor was swamped by darkness as they stepped into the dungeon. Slippery damp cobblestones covered the floor as the party walked over to the far side of the chamber, three cell doors stood before them. A simple bolt held one of the doors shut from the outside, while the other two doors were open. Edrik pointed and Damien brought the torch from the stair. Holding it up to a grill in the door, Edrik peered through to see a single figure crouched in the corner.

'Ackron, Ackron, it's Edrik, can you hear me?' The figure moved with a grunt and muffled moan. Edrik carefully slid the bolt to release the door. Hedoth and Edrik moved in to examine Ackron.

'Ackron, we are getting you out of here, can you stand?' said Edrik, Ackron nodded, raised his arms and was helped to his feet by both of them. 'Drink some of this.' offering a small water skin to Ackron's lips he drank. Akron's face was bruised and dirty, dried blood encrusted over one eyebrow. Hedoth put away the water skin as Ackron slumped between him and the Edrik, hanging by both arms. They walked him around the brazier a few times to try to warm him up, if it made a difference it didn't show.

'That's all the time we can afford.' Whispered Edrik, well aware of how long they had spent inside the castle.

'Shelaine, lead the way back, Tom and Damien take the rear.'

Shelaine guided them back up the stairwell, slightly quicker than before, the dampness faded as the smell of leather and sweat grew stronger. This time they were not as careful, they were making more noise and it was risky, nevertheless they pushed on up the stairs. Beeswax mixed with leather as they approached the great hall, sweet and fresh replacing stale and earthy. The aromas were almost overpowering in such a heightened state of alertness. Reaching the second floor Shelaine stepped into the clerk's hall filled with tall desks. At that precise moment the side door swung open and the tall figure of a guard holding a lamp stepped out of the room. Shelaine flinched a hand behind her back and a silver shard flew across the hall. The oil lamp smashed to the floor closely followed by the lifeless body the guard. Shelaine ran forward and calmly pulled her knife from the guard's forehead. After wiping it clean on his tunic she placed it back in its scabbard.

'To the window now!' Ordered Edrik, as he passed Akron to the warrior on guard. Hedoth and the warrior led Ackron through to the window.

'Get him outside and get on your way, quickly.'

Rumblings could be heard from above and below, as Akron was bundled through the window and onto the thatched roof. The noise of the guard hitting the floor was enough to attract attention, Edrik was knew what was coming next.

'Shelaine, fetch the torch, you two drag those desks over to the stairwell, we need to slow them down.' Edrik began grabbing armfuls of charts and other papers to start a fire. The guard's lamp was still burning and oil had started to spread across the floor, Tom and Damien franticly stacked three heavy desks against the opening of the stairwell. There was no door, but a fire might give them enough time to get Ackron back to the grain store at least. As a fourth desk crashed down onto the others Shelaine threw the torch onto the charts beneath. Edrik kicked the fallen lamp across the floor and into the stack of desks. Flaming oil sprayed out across the room as the lamp smashed against the desks and the staircase beyond. Edrik now ordered them all into the clerk's office, closing the door behind them. Wedging a chair and heavy desk up behind it they each in turn scrambled out of the window. Outside, nothing had changed, whatever chaos was beginning to form inside the keep had yet to show itself beyond the walls.

Hedoth and another warrior eased Ackron from the roof and passed him down to the warriors waiting below. The two of them followed and waited in the shadows for Edrik and the remainder to arrive. Ackron's' feet hardly touched the ground as his warriors rushed him back towards the grain store.

One by one the remainder scrambled from the window and ran across the roof. Edrik came last as smoke was now beginning to bellow from the window. Shelaine and the boys dropped to the ground as Hedoth and the last warrior waited to catch them.

'Run to the store and keep guard until we reach you.' Instructed Hedoth. They ran as close to the shadows of the wall as they could.

Ackron's group were now well inside the grain store,

scrambling through the tunnel, pushing and pulling him through the outer castle wall. Shelaine, Tom and Damien ducked inside the store and watched as Hedoth and the final warrior helped Edrik down from the roof. As Edrik hit the ground the massive doors of the keep burst open and shouts of 'fire' echoed out from within. A scattering of half-dressed guards stumbled down the keep steps, bewildered they ran toward the buildings on the far side of the courtyard beside the tavern. Chaos had erupted, fortunately on the opposite side of the castle for now.

Edrik's party ran past the round tower as its door swung open and a guard came running down the steps. A look of shock appeared on his face to see three warriors of Thon before him, a split second later Hedoth's sword trust upwards and deep into the guards' chest. The guard dropped his spear and slumped backward holding his stomach. Hedoth, Edrik and the warrior ran toward the grain store as two more guards appeared to find their comrade bleeding and pointing towards Edrik. Damien could sense what was about to happen, he stepped out of the doorway, taking an arrow from its quiver, he notched it to the bowstring, drew back hard and high, then released. A guard stretched back, levelling his spear towards the running warriors as Damien's arrow flashed past Edrik striking hard against the stone steps of the round tower. A flash and deafening roar of thunder echoed throughout the courtyard, shards of stone blasted from the steps in all directions, as smoke filled the space where the guards once stood. Edrik grabbed Damien by the collar as he passed, dragging him back into the grain store,

'Well done boy, now get into the tunnel.'

Outside the castle wall there was little to indicate what was taking place within. Dogs in the distance could be heard barking at each other, but there was nobody to be seen just yet. Tom and Shelaine emerged from the tunnel and into the tannery, there was no sign of Ackron and the two warriors. The doors to the tannery were open, indicating that Ackron had passed through, and so Tom and Shelaine waited for the others to catch up. One by one they appeared, scraping and scuffling their way through the tunnel. Without pause Edrik led them out of the tannery and back into the maze-like, claustrophobic alleyways. It was darker here, some noise could be heard from within the castle, but not enough to cause alarm beyond its menacing walls. Like six hunched rats they scampered through the alleyways and towards the waterwheel. Less cautious now than before, they splashed and squelched as they ran, shorter legs rushing to keep pace with the warriors. Then in the distance, the deep, haunting wail of a horn echoed out from beyond the towering castle walls, and then another. Dogs barked and confused murmurings began from within the huts around them.

Calls of 'Stand to arms! Stand to arms!' rang out from the gate house. Damien felt his heart drum heavy against his chest, he'd hardly taken a breath since the arrow left his bow, yet here he was almost sprinting now to keep up with the rest. The barking became louder as one by one the raiders dropped down onto the river bank. Still no chance to rest and still no sign of Ackron's party. Thoughts of failure and fear raced through Tom's mind as he forced them aside with positives *they were ahead, they had to be ahead of them.* Once on the riverbed, Edrik stepped aside to allow the rest through.

'Quickly, keep moving, keep moving.' urged Edrik as each one of them passed by. He took up position at the rear of the line as they continued their way upstream and further away from the chaos erupting behind them. The noise of the water now engulfed the sounds from the castle.

Damien couldn't help but check back to be sure they were not being followed. Not hearing was almost as bad as not seeing, he wanted to know what was happening, yet knew it would put them at greater risk.

'There, up ahead!' Hedoth was now leading the group with Edrik at the rear. In the distance Hedoth could see three figures struggling to make their way along the river bank, within minutes they were reunited. The warriors had made good ground, just a hundred paces or so from the treeline.

'Swap over!' Edrik motioned towards Hedoth and the remaining warrior to take hold of Ackron and give the other two warriors a rest. A brief pause to catch their breath was all it took, not long enough for the sweat to turn cold or the blisters to throb. Tom took a long glug from his water bottle and offered it to Shelaine, she politely shook her head, looking just as fresh and composed as when they first set out. Tom stuffed the bottle back into his pack, leant into his shoulder straps and continued.

Reaching the treeline, they clambered out of the riverbed and into the cover of the forest.

'OK, let's rest here for a few moments.' Edrik motioned them towards a clearing, set slightly back from the edge of the forest. He crouched and scanned the ground between himself and the distant castle, scrutinising every potential spot of cover, and analysing every movement.

'It doesn't look as though we have been noticed or followed, but they will realise, after the chaos has calmed down, that this wasn't accidental, and they will know where to point the blame.'

While they rested there in the cool dampness of the forest Edrik examined Ackron. He was very weak, his face swollen and bruised, speckled with dirt and dried blood from the horrors he'd been subjected to. Ackron reached out, resting a hand on Edrik's arm he whispered.

'Thank you, I will never forget this my friend.'

Edrik took Ackron's arm and placed it back by his side.

'Rest my good friend.'

The two of them had grown up together, close friends and excellent warriors, they were reunited again, and this strengthened their bond, together they were invincible.

Shelaine sat at the edge of the forest, looking back at the way they came. Gentle rolling hills embraced the stream as it threaded its way through the stillness of the meadow. Smoke rose upwards from the castle, now more cloud-like in its appearance, steam combined with smoke indicating the fire was under control and the cause of it would soon be uncovered. She turned to Edrik.

'We should leave soon; the fire has been put out.'

Edrik turned to Shelaine, nodded, and without question instructed the party to prepare to move out. Shelaine was observant, she was good and could be relied upon. The party got to their feet again and slowly, triumphantly began the march back to camp.

Chapter 13
Reunited

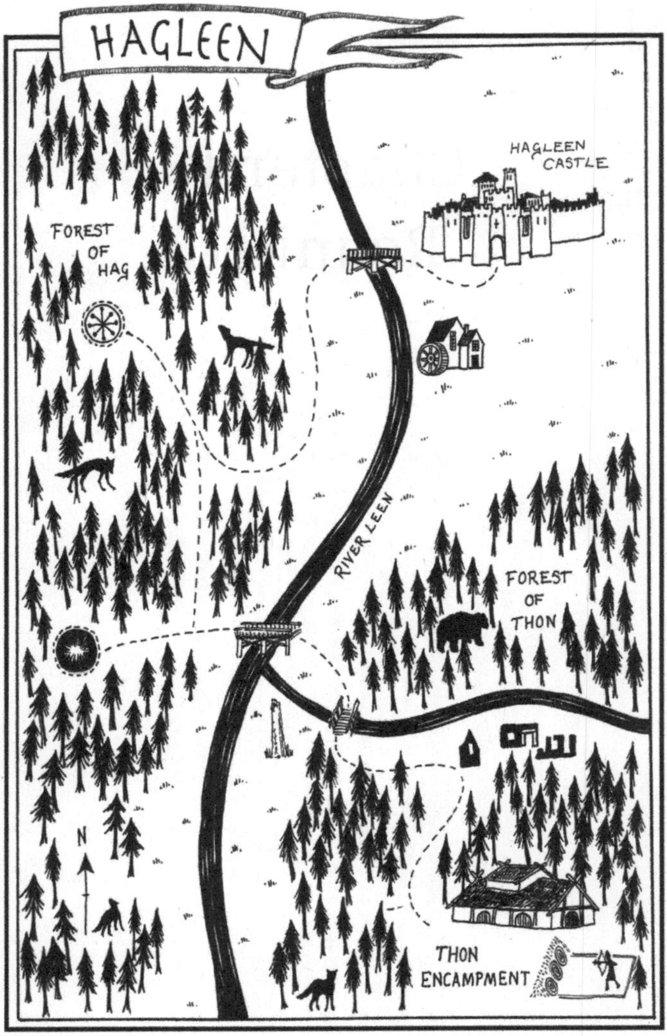
HAGLEEN
HAGLEEN CASTLE
FOREST OF HAG
RIVER LEEN
FOREST OF THON
N
THON ENCAMPMENT

Kneeling by his son's bed the Chief gazed upon Akron, tears glossing in his eyes.

'Akron, it's your father, you are safe again my boy, rest soundly, we will soon take back our home.' The Chief pressed his lips to Akron's forehead, heaved himself to his feet and turned towards the door. His giant, bear-like figure filling the door frame as he stepped through. Two guards either side of the hut braced themselves upright as he passed.

'Guard him well my boys.'

'Yes my Lord.'

Squelching along the track the Chief made his way to the sound of laughter and celebration. The large wooden feasting hall stood lit up by flaming torches at the doors. Two more guards braced themselves as the Chief stepped into the hall. A deafening cheer bellowed out from within. Mead, ale and food were plentiful as the Chief made his way through the boisterous, crowded hall. He stepped up onto a raised wooden platform and turned to face his warriors.

'My son has returned, and soon we begin our journey to retake this kingdom which is rightfully ours!'

The hall shook with a warlike chant.

'Thon! Thon! Thon!'

'Bring forth my warriors!' The Chief roared again.

A shout rang out and the hall doors opened, in strode Edrik followed by Hedoth, Shelaine, Tom, Damien and the three warriors who accompanied them. The hall splashed with ale as cheers rang out, deafening the warriors as they entered, making their way through the crowds towards the Chief.

'I'm beginning to get used to this.' shouted Damien halting before the steps of the podium.

The Chief raised a hand to settle the crowd. 'The Kingdom

of Thon once ruled these lands fairly, with compassion for our Elders, care for our sick and reward for our heroes.' The Chief glanced down at the eight warriors standing before him. 'Our Kingdom was ravaged by the Yarromites, torn apart by that barbaric race, they took all that they could from us, but they will never take our identity, our pride or our freedom!'

The crowd roared again with cheers of support.

'Today, the first step has been taken in regaining that which was stolen from our ancestors!'

Again, the crowd erupted in triumph.

'We have launched the first spear into the heart of our enemy, and we have many more ready to follow. Tonight, we celebrate this first blow by recognising our heroes, the courage and skills of these eight warriors will not go unnoticed. It is my privilege to reward each of them with the highest honour that can be bestowed on any warrior of Thon. The mark of the Warrior Knights of Thon!'

The crowd cheered, Edrik turned to Hedoth eyes wide, he could not believe his own ears. This was indeed the most prestigious honour any warrior could attain, few ever lived to receive it, it was often awarded to the dead for extreme courage in battle, and now he was about to receive what few had ever lived to receive.

'A Knighthood! That's cool, I wonder if we'll get some land to go with it?' Shouted Damian over the cheering.

'A holiday home in Dornachrov is enough for me, I like the thought of becoming a Knight though!' Replied Tom.

The Chief stepped aside as two warriors walked slowly across the podium carrying a brazier filled with glowing coals. Suspended on two carrying poles, they lowered the brazier to stand on its three iron feet in the centre of the podium. The Elder stepped forward from behind a large hanging curtain to the rear of the hall. Carrying a long branding iron with a symbol crafted into the iron tip, he placed it into the red-hot coals and stepped back.

'Bring wine!' Shouted the Chief and immediately the heroes were given large goblets of wine filled from a barrel. 'Drink hard warriors, you are about to become Knights!' The hall shook with cheer as they drank to their achievement.

'If mum could see us now, Warrior Knights of Thon.' Said Tom.

'She'd kick your ass for drinking under age, besides, we're not Knights yet, we haven't been awarded our medals.' Laughed Damien.

'Do you think we get medals?'

'Yeah! Knights always get medals. Maybe a sword or some other weapon too, or even a horse!' Said Damien.

'A fricking horse! You can't even ride a bike!' Laughed Tom

The Chief stepped forward 'Now for the ceremony, step forward, warrior Edrik.' Edrik stepped forward and offered up his right forearm. The Elder raised the branding iron and spoke.

'In the name of Thon, I declare you Edrik Warrior Knight of Thon.' The Elder pressed the iron onto Edrik's flesh causing it to hiss and smoked as the iron made its mark. Edrik's face was red with sweat, teeth clenched as he was led off to the side and his arm thrust in a barrel of cold water. Cheers erupted through the hall turning into roars as a Knight of Thon was made.

'Holy shit! Mums going to go frickin ape!' Tom said, turning to face Damien just in time to see him slump to the ground.

Shelaine turned to see what the clatter was, finding Damien collapsed having fainted 'What's wrong with him?'

'I don't think he's too keen on getting branded.' replied Tom as he knelt down to lift up his friend with the help of a warrior.

The sickly stench of burning flesh now filled the hall as one by one the triumphant warriors moved forward to offer their flesh to the scarlet kiss of iron. Tom felt his arm vanish with searing pain as the skin fried under the heat of the branding iron, he felt a deep sickness in his stomach as the iron was removed and he stepped to the water barrel. Seering pain lanced through his arm turning to numbness as he plunged it into the barrel. He looked up to see Damien, still unconscious and held up by a warrior on either side like an offering to the Elder. As the iron touched his skin Damien awoke with a scream, the two warriors carried him to join to his friend, plunging his arm into the icy water. Shelaine nodded to the Chief and offered her forearm to the Elder. The iron bit hard yet not a glimpse of pain or fear showed on her face. As she approached the barrel a single tear slid gracefully to the roundness of her smooth chin then held there until falling to the ground. Shelaine placed a hand on Damien's shoulder, pulled him close and kissed his cheek. She whispered something to which Damien replied 'Thank you.' through a damp mess of tears and sobbing.

One by one the remaining warriors were made into Knights. Celebrations took hold, warriors sloshed ale and mead, stumbling in drunkenness singing battle songs and howling cheers. The pain was killed by drink and dizziness until song turned to silences and voices disappeared into the darkness beyond the doors.

Tom awoke with a head three times its usual weight,

then immediately vomited in the corner of the hall. Every inch of his body pounded with pain as he searched half doubled over looking for water.

'Here, drink this.' Croaked a gravelled voice, an old and withered hand offered him a small cup of liquid. 'Don't sip it, drink it all in one.'

Tom did as he was instructed, the liquid was strong in flavour, but not unpleasant, he swallowed it down. Tom handed back the cup, thanking the old man realising it was the Elder who had branded them the night before.

'I imagine it's still very painful.' pointing at the bright red wound on Tom's arm. 'When your friends are awake, I will remedy that, and then I will show you all to your lodgings.'

'Lodgings?' Asked Tom, still clutching his stomach.

'Yes, we were going to give you each a small place, but as you don't yet have families, we thought it might get lonely.' Placing the cup in his shoulder bag the Elder continued. 'You've been allocated a single large dwelling house with a servant to take care of your needs. Of course, as you get older you may wish to take a partner and so this will be reconsidered when appropriate.' The Elder smiled then turned to make his way through the scattering of bodies and clutter strewn throughout the hall. 'Bring the others when they awake, my hut is beside that of the Chief, it's the one with the skulls hanging above the door.' Tom nodded then began to look around for Damien.

'A servant! A bloody servant, me?' Said Damien.

'Well not just you, they will take care of all three of us.'

'Oh man! This is getting insane; will they fetch us food and tidy up and stuff?'

'I've never had a servant myself Damie, but I'm guessing so.' Grinned Tom. 'Don't forget we still have to get back to Dornachrov yet, we might not live to see that house!

Anyway, c'mon we need to find the Elder, he's going to give us something for the pain.'

'You need to work on your aim.' Said a voice from behind.

Damien looked around to see Shelaine carefully honing the blade of her knife.'

'That bow and those arrows are very useful tools, but you need to work on those skills of yours if you want to get better use out of them.'

Tom smirked, 'She's right, we both need to learn how to use these weapons or we might not get the chance to enjoy that house and servant. Can you teach us?'

'Let's find the Elder first and then see if there's anything left of that archery range'.

The sky was grey and heavy, thick with wood smoke and not a breath of wind to clear it. As they approached the hut the Elder called them in. Inside it was dark, a fire pit burned in the centre. The stench of herbs was heavy, swirling wood smoke and sweet incense combined to trigger the senses into a magical, spiritual atmosphere.

'Sit on the bench by the table and hold out your forearms.' They sat side by side as the Elder came forward with a small bowl and a wooden spoon. They watched as his skeletal fingers stirred the spoon in the bowl then gently pasted the contents over each wound. The ointment was thick and cold as it touched the skin, and as it did, a numbness spread across the area, instantly dulling the fiery pain of the burn. The Elder placed the bowl on the table behind them then picked up some dried moss and bandages. Carefully placing the moss over the ointment then binding and tying off each bandage.

'That should help for a day or two, come back when the pain returns and I shall redress the wounds.' With a warm and caring smile, the Elder stepped back as Shelaine and the boys thanked him then ducked out of the hut.

Dampness and dew lingered into late morning as the trio trudged their way along the track to the archery range. Shelaine pulled two bread rolls out of her shoulder bag and handed them to the boys. 'Here, these might help soak up that hangover.' They took them and each began to eat as they walked, the bread was soft and sweet as they chewed, washing it down with water.

Other than a couple of guards on the outskirts of the village there were few people around. After the previous night's celebrations it was a quiet day, one for focusing more on recovery than anything else. They continued down the track and past the barracks. Entering the range Shelaine selected a bow and quiver of arrows from a line of wooden racks filled with a selection of ranged weapons. Tom and Damien did the same and all three stood facing the target area some sixty paces or so ahead of them.

'Let's try a longer distance today, if you hit something too close with those arrows you are more likely to kill yourself.' Shelaine took an arrow from her quiver. 'Don't spend too long thinking, use your strength to do the work, but don't strain and don't hold too long. Each part of your body must work to support the other, notch, draw, aim, release.' Shelaine loosed an arrow down range striking the centre of her target. 'Maintain focus on the task and be aware of what is around you, notch, draw, aim, release.' She loosed a second arrow striking the target alongside her first. 'For now, don't think of accuracy, think of consistency, do it the same every time. Notch, draw, aim, release.' She released a third arrow which slammed in between the others.

Shelaine was good, she knew exactly what she was doing, and with smooth delicate skill released three more arrows in rapid succession, each striking hard into the distant target. Tom looked at Damien to see his eyes widen, he turned to face his target as they both began the process of placing an arrow on the bowstring.

'Together, follow my timing, notch, draw, aim, release. Notch, draw, aim, release. Notch, draw, aim, release.'

Arrows began to cascade down the range at random intervals, with little accuracy or consistency.

'Don't think about accuracy at this stage, pick a spot in the distance, the height of a human above your target and try to find rhythm, notch, draw, aim, release.'

She slowly tapped her bow on the wooden floor to provide a beat the boys could match. After five minutes a lozenge shape of white feathers had appeared down range before each of them. Some had gone very short or off to the side, but most had gathered toward the middle.

'Now stop and look forward, the white feathered patch is your killing zone, or grouping, the better you get, the smaller this group will be. Both of you are shooting too low, aim higher. Now go forward and collect your arrows, we'll try again.'

Shelaine kept them there all afternoon, repeating the process, but taking rests as their forearms ached with bruises from strikes of the bow string. Gradually their grouping became tighter and the distance greater. The following day they focused on using swords and knives, even a small group of warriors came down to watch and learn, word had begun to get out of how skilled a warrior this young girl was.

As the days went on, Ackron grew stronger and began to take more of a role in running the camp, he too attended the training sessions led by Shelaine, and instructed groups of warriors to attend advanced training along with Tom and Damien. A strong-fighting warrior force was now turning elite, and soon it would be time to support

Dornachrov in its defence against the Yarromites. Tom and Damien became more skilled and more accurate, they trained daily with Shelaine, and after weapon training would go out on arduous raiding or hunting parties. Day by day increasing their skills, confidence and status amongst the other warriors.

'You might be a good shot, but you need to be a little more cautious when crossing streams.' Shelaine laughed closing her door as she stepped into the main room of their lodgings. Damien finished hanging his wet jeans up by the hearth, his face reddened as he realised he was only wearing shorts. 'No need to be embarrassed, you're sweet Damien, but you're not my type.' Shelaine laughed.

'Nice to know!' Damien replied awkwardly, quickly covering himself with a blanket then sitting on a low bench by the fire. The bench was thickly padded out with warm blankets and furs. He began rubbing his feet dry with a small towel. The dwelling they were given consisted of a large hall with a fire place in the centre, surrounding it were low benches with high backs and sides to keep out any draft. Around the sides of the hall stood several rough-cut pieces of furniture, a sideboard on which rested various drinking tankards, plates and a pottery water jug. By the door was a weapon rack supporting three tall spears together with a selection of swords and bows. Four huge oak chairs stood around a heavy dining table, and over the fire hung a blackened cooking pot on a tripod. The far end of the hall had been partitioned into three rooms, one for each of the occupants. They had spent several weeks living and training in Thon, and by now were anticipating an order to prepare for departure.

Tom cluttered into the hall, dripping wet from the rain outside. He loosened the collar of a heavy cape and hung it to dry on the back of the door. Damien was now drying his boots by the fire while Shelaine carefully fitted a new bowstring to one of her hunting bows beside him. 'I was speaking with Edrik this morning; he's expecting an order to move at some point over the next two days. Looks like we are going to battle soon.' Said Tom.

'Excellent, I could use some excitement, well, once my jeans are dry that is!'

'Don't be so keen Damien, this will be much harder than the raid on Hagleen Castle.' Replied Shelaine.

'He just wants to get back to Herran, I think she has a soft spot for him.' Laughed Tom.

'Herran! She's not interested in me! She fixed me up well, but that was it. It was the sweetbread I was thinking about.'

The three of them laughed as Tom placed a couple more logs onto the fire, crackling and hissing they spat orange speckles skyward, vanishing in the smoky air above. Crimson embers from the fire radiated their heat throughout the hall with a warm sleepiness, reddening cheeks and weighing down eyelids as the dampness slowly dried. Tom sat beside Damien and stared into the hypnotic flames of the fire, delicately weaving their finger-like torches around the bark of fresh logs. After a few moments all three of them were dozing, as the dampness turned to brittle hot dryness and the fire softly whispered them to sleep.

Chapter 14
Mission to Devlon

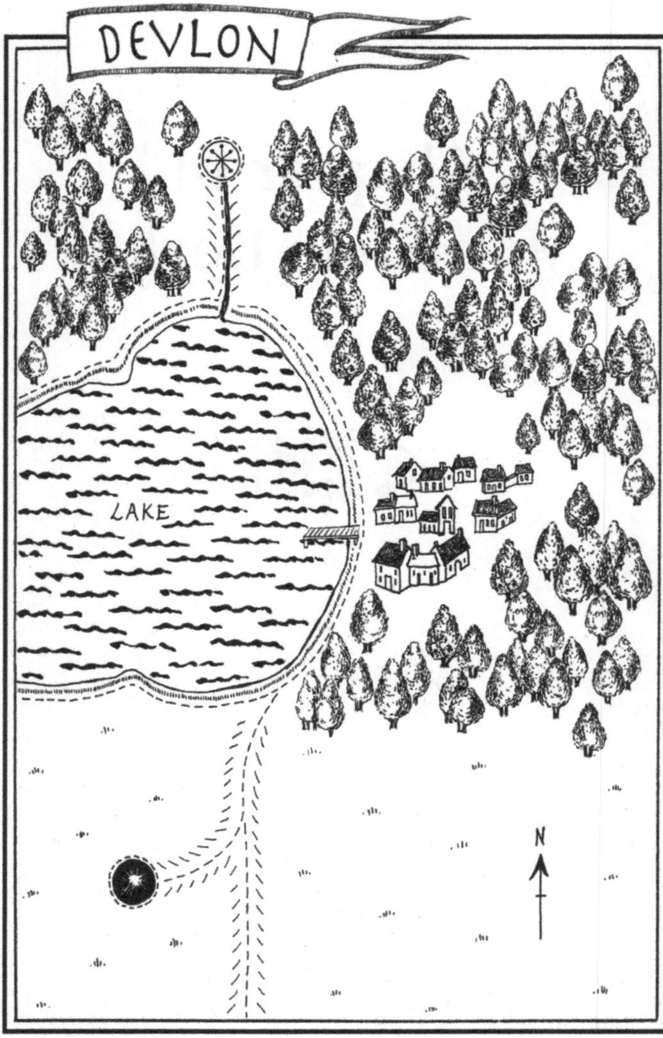
DEVLON
LAKE
N

Burwell's horse bowed against its reigns as it stood holding the weight of its rider. Black and pristinely groomed, it looked formidable against the greyness of the stone-walled gatehouse beyond. To his left stood six more beautiful black horses, each carrying a Yarromite cavalryman. Blackened steel breastplates fitted over black tunics, embellished with fine silver and red piping down the sleeve and trouser leg. Each cavalryman was armed with a sabre hanging loosely from the waist, with a short black bow slung to the side of his horse. The finest troops that the Yarromite army had to offer.

Conrach approached, mounted on Nelly, a chestnut mare, Burwell gestured a nod as Nelly trotted comfortably across the cobbles to join the troop.

'This way Commander, to the old fort. I hope you brought something to cover that' Conrach muttered, frowning over the breastplate armour 'we don't want to look too much like a cavalry unit.'

'Of course Elder, the men have oilskins to blend in.' Burwell brought his horse close by Conrach and instructed his Sergeant of Horse to direct the troop to follow on. The old fort lay two miles west of the city, in its day it was a vast fortification, laid out around the passing circle. Surrounding the fortified walls were barracks to house a thousand strong army, an army whose only purpose was to be dispatched to raid other lands. The route to the old fort was once a well-trodden path, a cobbled road easily wide enough for twelve horses. Over many years the Yarromites would send troops of cavalry and regiments of foot soldiers to pilfer treasures, weapons and resources. Back and forth from strange lands to Yarromovia, outposts were established along with bridgeheads in each land, built to enable the systematic processing of stolen wealth and resources. The most brutal of crimes involved the taking of slaves from every nation, the strong were enslaved into transporting, building and all manner of labour. Anyone who proved difficult was murdered, man, woman or child. The Yarromites cared only for themselves, any other race was either used as an asset or seen as a risk, and then processed accordingly.

The going was easy, a broad cobbled road cutting through the forest as straight as the terrain would allow. Over the years the might of the forest had begun to reclaim that road, tree roots forcing upward to raise the cobbles. Ivy and brambles creeping wherever the sunlight enticed them to, stretching to meet with the apple green canopy above. Cobblestones, covered with a soft carpet of leaves and detritus, cushioning to silence the iron hooves as they trod the ground beneath them. Above, a shelter of greenery for the troops as they walked a route which thousands like them walked before.

'Tell me Elder, how did you come by this book?'

'That's a good question Commander.' Conrach leant back in his saddle, content to be sharing his wisdom. 'Many years ago, this book resided in the great vaults of the passing circle, the place we are going to right now. When the powers of the book ceased there was no reason to keep it there, nor any reason to maintain the garrison there either. The Elder of that time was tasked with securing the book and ensuring the emperor was informed immediately if its powers ever returned. Each Elder passed down the book, its knowledge and the responsibility.' Conrach paused, and with an air of grandeur continued 'I, Commander Burwell, am the chosen Elder, the one to take on that responsibility for the Empire of Yarromovia!'

Burwell ignored the grandiose posturing, he was a fighter, and a trophy hunter. He had little interest in the Empire, he wanted wealth, and if this old fool could find him and his troops that, then he was happy to follow. 'I was aware of the old fort and some legend of travelling to far off lands, but I never thought it to be true.' Said Burwell.

'Oh, it is very much true Commander, but there is now a risk. You see there are three of these books, and we have no knowledge of who possess the other two. Certainly, the Creghelt possess one I'm sure of that, but the whereabouts of the other book is a mystery. The keepers of that book could well pose a threat to Yarromovia.' Conrach's tone changed to one of caution. 'We must be ready Commander! When we return from our raid we won't come back this way, we will come through what's known as the portal. That portal must be guarded; it is a weak spot into Yarromovia.'

'Leave the defences to me Elder, there isn't an army alive that can match the might of Yarromovia!'

'I'm sure of that Commander, but the portal must be defended against invasion. The Yarromites have made many enemies over the centuries, and I suspect we shall make many more.' Both Conrach and Burwell laughed as they trotted on. The path before them began to slope gently downward, and with it a shallow mist began to blanket the ground. In the distance the old gate house slowly came into view, like a stone shipwreck on a powder-grey sea of mist. A huge arched door frame stood in the centre of the gatehouse, its gigantic oak doors now hanging loosely and precariously to either side. The ground, now obscured by shallow mists, as the horses walked silently through, their nostrils adding to the clouds beneath them.

'Commander, instruct each of your troop to grasp the reigns of the rider in front. We don't want anyone bolting off at the sight of what is about to happen.'

Burwell looked over and nodded to his Sergeant of Horse

who, in turn, checked each rider understood.

Conrach led them to the centre of a huge square courtyard, around its edges stood the remains of barrack buildings, stores, blacksmiths and armouries, all now ghostlike and skeletal in appearance, time had softened their edges while the elements had pounded their rooftops inward. Reaching inside his coat, Conrach pulled out the book as the troop came to a halt in the centre. Resting the spine of the book on the pommel of his saddle he checked the map to see the cross in the centre of the passing circle. Conrach then slowly turned the pages, examining each title, he could feel his pulse growing stronger with every page as beads of sweat began to roll down his forehead.

'Devlon.' he muttered, then turning to the cavalry he awkwardly raised himself up in his saddle.

'Prepare yourselves gentlemen, you are about to enter the history books of Yarromovia. Our Empire has not travelled for hundreds of years, but now we ride again.' His somewhat pathetic figure didn't match the energy of his speech, but he continued. 'Under the banners of our ancestors at the orders of His Highness the Imperial Emperor of Yarromovia, this honour is ours gentlemen!'

'Long live the Empire!' Shouted the Sergeant of Horse.

'The Empire!' Bellowed out the troopers in response, an infamous battle cry preceding death and slaughter, a battle cry the Yarromites were renowned for on an immeasurable scale.

Standing to one side, Conrach raised the book and began to recite its words.

'Elders of the book of Cregheligan,
we seek channel to Devlon,
through worlds afar,
part the elements,

part time and space,
through the void of existence grant this journey.'

As Conrach finished those last words, to the fading sounds of cheer the light dimmed and the mists began to rise. Horses unsettled as their world fell from view, the colours surrounding them washed into one another, forming new shapes and patterns as the ground beneath their hooves rippled and vibrated. Leaving the mists and buildings of Yarromovia behind, the sound of birdsong filled the air and a sweet aroma of summertime breezed in. Fresh green meadow grass was the first to appear, then the warmth and openness of the fields around them. They had arrived in Devlon on a hillside in summertime, with nothing but the faintest of a breeze and tranquillity before them.

Riders desperately regained control of their horses and their own senses after the experience of the portal. As both gradually began to calm down, Conrach opened the book to the map page and inspected their whereabouts. Precisely as planned, the book had delivered them to the location listed on his ancient charts, he grinned excitedly then pointed.

'There Commander, we need to head for the bottom of that valley. There should be a lake beyond that hill and a small town on the banks of that lake. Not too big, but large enough to offer up a few trinkets and souvenirs to take back. Once we have all we need, the way home is on the far side of the lake.'

'Excellent, then let us waste no more time here than we need to, Sergeant lead on!'

'Yes Sir!'

This time the cavalry troop moved more swiftly, a steady trot in twos they filed, with the Sergeant in front, Burwell and Conrach remained at the rear. Inevitably there would be bloodshed, yet without a battle, this raid was about to end the stillness of summer for one small town in Devlon.

At the base of the hill the Sergeant halted the troop, they each covered their uniforms and weapons by draping oilskin capes over their shoulders. The Sergeant then ordered the troop to break formation before joining a cart track, and slowly the lake came into view. Keeping a casual pace, they followed the track towards the shore, curving to the right the town came into view. In the distance, children could be seen launching tiny boats into the lake, several townsfolk looking on as they sat beneath a line of trees by the shoreline. Nobody noticed as the group drew closer, either sleeping or too preoccupied to see, to them it was just another a lazy summers day.

The first building the troop encountered was a large grey stone house, its roof was crenelated to appear as a castle battlement, topped with a square tower to one side. The Sergeant ordered the troop to halt and dismount, each pulling empty sacks from saddlebags and tucking them into belts or tunics. A decorative wooden gate and hedgerow formed the boundary to the ornate property, until a riding boot kicked it through, splintering as it fell into the rose garden beyond. Conrach and Burwell looked on as the troop forced their way through the front door. Boots fell silent on finely woven carpet, as they looted their way through the home. A door led off to the left of the hallway and was swiftly kicked open in desperation to find wealth. Beyond the door was a large drawing room, a sideboard and mantlepiece lay adorned with a mixture fine pottery ornaments and silverware. Sacks began to fill with plunder as the troops frenzied on the sights.

The thumping of boots could be heard disappearing

to the upper floors. Then a scream shrilled out and was quickly muffled, followed by the deadweight thud of something heavy falling to the floor, the boots continued. Thuggishly riffling through possessions, scattering and scouring their way through what did not belong to them, a ring here, pocket watch there, every trinket was taken and every cupboard explored.

Conrach and Burwell maintained their presence outside the building, with one trooper holding the rest of the horses. The sounds from within were muffled, even the scream could have been mistaken for the call of a crow. They looked on at the children playing by the water's edge, two had noticed the strange people on horseback with more horses alongside, but this gave them no cause for alarm, and so they continued to enjoy themselves.

'Tell me Elder, what plans do you have for this book, surely there is far more than a few ornaments to be had with it?'

'Far more indeed Commander, the powers of this book ceased many years ago, by that time we had established outposts in other worlds. These worlds need to be reunited with Yarromovia.'

'Do we know why the powers ceased?'

'No, but we do know there are two more books, and if we could obtain these, they would help secure our borders, and increase our capacity to expand.'

The first of the troops bundled out of the doorway, a hessian sack slung over his shoulder, heaving it through the gate he tied it to the saddle of his horse and mounted. Another followed, then another and one by one the horses were loaded.

'How goes it, Sergeant?'

'All well Sir, very little resistance.'

'Good good, do we have room for a few passengers?'

'Passengers Sir?' Replied the Sergeant.

Burwell gestured towards the children playing by the water's edge. 'I'm sure the Emperor would approve of some extra servants!' Laughed Burwell.

The last two troopers made their way out of the doorway and once their sacks had been fastened to their horses the Sergeant beckoned them over. After a few words they both grinned in unison, mounted their horses and trotted over to the two children.

Conrach studied the map, the Sergeant ordered his men to the road to casually start making their way around the lake.

'We should leave now Elder, to the other side of the lake you say?'

'Yes.' Replied Conrach, pointing a stumpy ink-stained finger towards the base of a valley on the far side of the lake.

'Then let's make haste, for it might begin to get lively around here.'

Conrach tucked away the book and kicked back hard on his spurs. His horse bolted to life just behind Burwell's as the troop held back at the rear.

The village was serene, just a handful of buildings standing proudly, set back from the lake's edge and warming in the afternoon sunshine. A scene of honey bees sipping sweetness from well-tended garden flowers, the occasional butterfly commuting from bloom to bloom. Between each house ran a lane reaching back to the main part of the village beyond, had the intruders dared to explore further they might have noticed the elaborately carved stone fountain in the centre of the square, or the ornate sculptures which surrounded it. These gems were not seen, they could not have been plundered and so would serve no purpose to the Yarromites who thieved, murdered and abducted their way through this beautiful place.

'That's a nice dolly young lady, I wonder if she's ever been on a horse?' Two horsemen dismounted and approached a young boy and girl beside the lake. The innocent minds around them saw nothing of the soldiers' intent, as they chatted warmly with the children.

The rest of the troop passed by, several paces ahead as the playfully friendly chat continued. The two children happily enjoyed being hoisted up and into saddles, smiles appeared on the faces of onlookers, pleased by the friendliness of the horsemen. Then with a gentle tap of a spur the two horsemen slowly trotted off in the direction of the others. Speed was not necessary, for a simple trot around the lake was all that was offered.

Conrach and Burwell slowed to a trot as they approached the foot of the valley. Pulling out the book, Conrach checked the map, the passing circle was close by.

'Just a short way up the valley from here Commander, we should allow the others to catch up.' Conrach placed the book back into his jacket and fumbled in his pocket for an old wooden pipe. With a small knife he scraped out the blackened tobacco from the bowl of the pipe, tapping it carefully on the pommel of his saddle. Tiny flakes of burnt tobacco ash fell softly, swirling around in the faint breeze towards the ground. Taking out an old leather pouch of rich, sweet-smelling pipe tobacco he pulled out a pinched and rubbed it in the palm of his hand. He then filled the pipe bowl, stuffing down the moist fresh leaf with a finger, stained brown from years of similar use. Placing the pipe to the left side of his mouth he held it between his teeth while returning the pouch and knife to his pocket. The fumbling began again; this time he took out a small tinderbox. Pushing off the lid to reveal thick shard of flint, a steel and some cotton tinder wick. Conrach began to strike the steel against the flint until the soft cotton wick began to glow, a pearl of orange shone from its softness. Conrach blew on the wick before offering it up to the pipe. Clouds of fragrant pipe smoke began to swirl around like a mystical fog, stubbing out the wick and closing the box he placed it back into his pocket.

The last two horsemen approached, Conrach pulled on the reins spurring his horse off to the right along a narrow track and through the valley. Burwell followed as the Sergeant instructed the troop follow on. Waiting for them to pass, the Sergeant looked around for followers then took up position at the rear. Still enjoying their ride, the children giggled and laughed with one another as the lake slowly disappeared from view.

The track through the valley was narrow and clear, the pace was casual and calm, as the horses trod the ground into mud beneath heavy hooves. Eyes wide with excitement, the children showed no concern as Conrach brought them to a halt.

'Join reins as before gentlemen!' Instructed Conrach as he wheeled the troop off the track and into a broad clearing. Once inside, Conrach turned to the last page of the book and recited the verse.

'Merwag ed Wroth!'

The ground began to shake, the horses unsettled and the children screamed, sounds distorted as the colours of the forest ran into each other once again, and the world of Yarromovia reappeared.

Chapter 15
March to Dornachrov

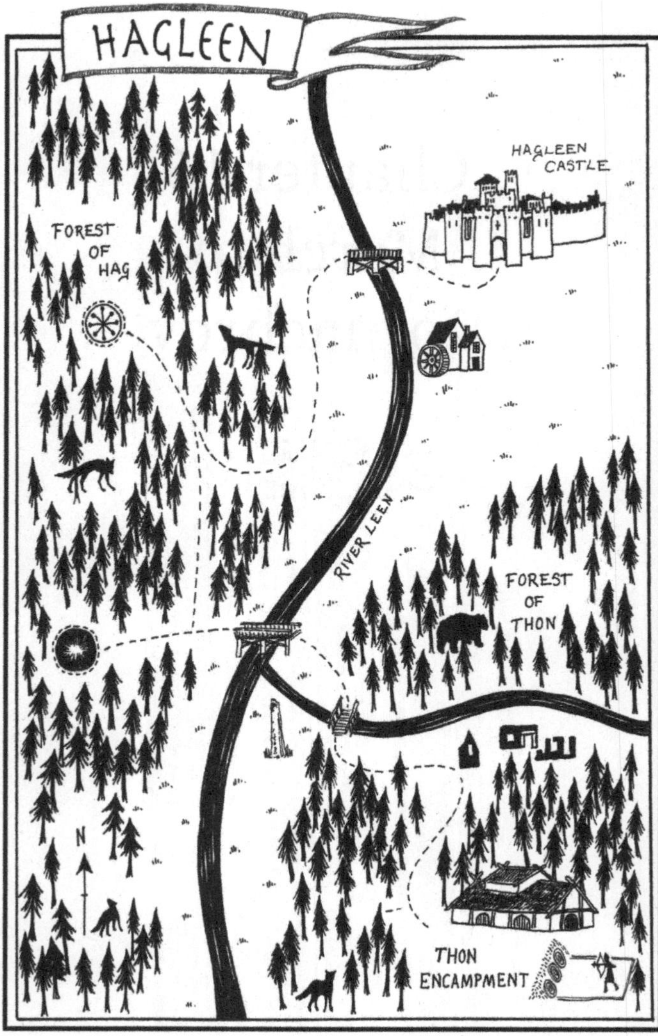
HAGLEEN
HAGLEEN CASTLE
FOREST OF HAG
RIVER LEEN
FOREST OF THON
N
THON ENCAMPMENT

The deep echo of a horn bellowed out through the village, followed by another. Tom woke with a shiver beside Damien, the logs in the fire had smouldered to a delicate grey skeleton of their former shape, ever so slightly offering the last of their warmth into the hall. Shelaine appeared from her room, fastening a belt around her waist. 'Sleep well? Looks like you were right Tom, today is the day we return to Dornachrov.' She said, walking towards the fire.

Damien yawned and rubbed his hands hard to force away the chill. 'It's not even dawn yet.' He replied.

'I'll ask the Chief if you can have a couple more hours.' Sniggering as she ladled out a spoon of broth from the pot above the fire. 'I think there's just enough left from last night if you guys want some?'

Tom jumped up, shivered, and grabbing a bowl followed suit, as Damien forced on his brittle jeans. The haunting moan of a horn sounded again followed by another, echoing through the valley. The three of them slurped down the remaining tepid broth, then swapping bowls for weapons they stepped into the silvery grey before dawn. Each wore the same clothes as the day they arrived, but with the addition of more practical embellishments. Thick fur waistcoats and long heavy capes to keep the rain from soaking through. The garb was good, but not fine, it gave them warmth against the cold and fitted well. The boys' rucksacks had now been replaced with more practical shoulder bags which they could wear under their capes to keep dry.

The wind was crisp and icy fresh as they joined the lines of warriors making their way to the bottom of the valley. It was hard to recognise familiars amongst the bear-shaped silhouettes, heavy with furs and fighting gear. The three of them weaved their way through these giants to the Chief's hut. Pushing back a large door and filtering through a heavy set of curtains. Inside they were met with the warmth of the firepit, it cradled flame caressed logs, hissing and spitting embers into the vastness of the room. The smell of burning wood filled the place and hung heavy like a cloud.

'Knights! Over here!' The Chief was standing beside Ackron, a large canvas map rolled out over the table before them.

'This is the route you need to take to reach the passing circle.' Pointing to a line drawn on the map. 'The route is old but still traceable, and you'll be familiar with some of it, as it'll take you close to the castle again.'

Tom noticed the path took them down to the river as before, but this time across it and up into the opposite forest. He was ready for excitement, and looking forward to seeing Dornachrov again, it had been several weeks now since they left the place. Hard to comprehend the change they had undergone since arriving at Thon.

'Ackron will lead the army this time, supported by Edrik, Hedoth and the three of you. We have six hundred warriors of Thon amassed to support the defence of Dornachrov, hopefully, with the addition of a few Ember pearl weapons that should suffice. Are there any questions?'

Shelaine, eyes fixed on the map glanced up at the Chief 'Is the passing circle likely to be guarded?'

'I shouldn't think so, many people know of its whereabouts as there was once an outpost close by' The Chief pointed to a few small huts marked on the map 'but I doubt there's anything left of that now. There shouldn't be any presence nearby to get in the way.'

Shelaine nodded and continued to scrutinise the map.

The Chief placed a hand on Ackron's shoulder 'I wish I could share this duty with you son, I place my trust in you and your sword, and with that I shall leave you to your work.' Ackron nodded then turned to Shelaine.

'I would like the three of you to join my warband at the head of the column, Captains Tulea and Karrell will lead the second and third warbands of archers, Borgas Captain of spear will form the fourth warband, and behind him will follow Reeval and Duntan each leading a warband of swords.' The captains each nodded acknowledging their orders. 'Captains ready your troops!'

The five Captains filed out of the hut and into the crisp grey dawn as Chief Egreth gave his son a bear hug and a heavy pat on the shoulder 'Gods of Thon be by your side son.'

Ackron led the remainder of the party outside and to the head of the first warband. This was Ackron's own band of warriors, heavy bear-like swordsmen of Thon. Each warband consisted of around one hundred warriors, some female and some male, they all fought together. Some were married and even fought beside their loved ones, in some cases their teenage offspring too. The only distinction were the archers, these units were made up entirely of women, no armour or shields, just light furs, a dagger, arrows, quivers and bows adorned these warriors. In Thon, women made better archers than men, they could shoot quicker and move faster. All warriors were trained in archery, but the better archers were always women, they were the elite ranged warrior. Tulea and Karrell each led a band of one hundred archers, they were like no other, they lived in their own part of the camp, away from the male warriors. The archers lived, ate and slept together as one community, their skills were second to none and highly respected by the other units.

Outside, the cold air pricked at faces as the group stepped out from the warmth of Egreth's hut. The darkness, now fringed with the greyness of an approaching dawn, as each Captain took up their position at the head of their respective columns. Chief Egreth stood at the doorway of his hut, a giant of a warrior draped in thick bearskins, beside him a young boy, the Chief raised a hand and the boy lifted a ram's horn to his lips and blew. The sharp sound echoed through the rank and file of the assembled army and beyond through the blackness of the forest, slowly they began to move off. The dampness of dawn now blended with the musk of furs and leather as the first column made its way along the track. Swords rumbled against wooden shields, muffled by leather scabbards, boots squelched and sucked at the mud beneath them as it gradually churned with every passing warrior.

Two columns of archers followed behind Ackron's band of warriors. The archers were nimble and carried less weight, making for a lighter, less cumbersome pace. A faint rattle of arrows emanated from packed quivers slung over shoulders. Each archer carried two slender quivers containing twelve arrows. Twenty-four arrows per archer, two thousand four hundred arrows per unit, and this was just their personal supply. Along with the archers were young warriors carrying extra supplies of arrows, bows and bowstrings. The archers, a formidable asset relying on speed and accuracy were not to be underestimated. They were held in high regard by their comrades as a reliable and deadly fighting force.

The spear bearers followed, led by Captain Duntan, a defensive unit, they mainly used their weapons to hold off attacking forces by jabbing rather than throwing. Occasionally a spear might get thrown if advancing on an enemy position, but it was risky, it left the warrior with little else to fight with. All warriors carried daggers, even the archers, but they were for very close combat and no match for a sword. Finally, two more bands of warrior swordsmen followed, the warbands of Captains' Borgas and Reeval. These would act as reserve and rear guard until reaching their destination.

Steam rose up from the serpent-like army of warriors as it twisted its way along the track. The torchlight of the village slipped away from view as fresh morning air changed its scent from one of wood smoke and cooking, to pine trees, sweat and damp furs. It felt warmer now that they were moving, as the crisp, silvered dawn began to colour itself orange. There was no talking or chatter from the ranks, just the low grumble of boots as they trod the ground beneath them. The shrill of birdsong surrounded them, piercingly intense. From the front of the column the occasional rabbit or deer would bolt away into the distance as this unfamiliar sight approached, and soon the sound of running water.

The narrow bridge across the stream came into view and Ackron ordered the army to halt. He moved forward with his Knights to check the area was clear. cautiously approaching they looked for signs of disturbance, all appeared to be untouched and so Ackron signalled the army to proceed in single file. Ackron led the way following the path along the stream. It was narrow and obscured with bracken in places, but easy to follow. By the time they reached the edge of the treeline the sun had at last risen and the crispness of dawn began to ebb away. The army was halted at the edge of the forest while the leaders went forward to check for danger. The all clear was given and each unit reformed into three ranks, weaving and slipping its way down the meadow to the river bank. At the bottom of the valley six hundred warriors gradually vanished into cover, as Ackron led the army slowly down the river towards the castle.

The air hung with a ghostly mist, hovering just above the stream, haunting in its presence. The river swept by gracefully with the odd trout rising, sucking up fallen insects from the surface in deeper places. The sound from the running water was louder than that of the warriors, but it also masked any sound from beyond its own banks. Damien found this unnerving, feeling relief when Ackron eventually raised a hand bringing the army to a halt. Shelaine checked the map, to find that they had reached the point where they now had to cross the stream and ascend to the forest on the opposite side of the valley.

Ackron led, followed by his Knights, their feet grew numb as they waded through the stream, it was only knee-deep, but it was cold and they would have to deal with this for the rest of the day. On reaching the opposite side they left the stream and began to climb the sandy clay bank of the river. The pace slowed as the meadow beyond the river became steeper. The cawing and cackle of crows sounded in the distance, gravelled tones of disapproval at their invaders. Lifting and beating their wings in slow motion as they gradually put distance between themselves and the warriors.

A snake of six hundred warriors twisted its way up the valley and into the distant forest. Looking back over his shoulder Tom could see the waterwheel and castle beyond, he knew they must be visible from the castle at this distance and he felt a certain sense of vulnerability in knowing they were probably being watched. Nothing could be done about that; the mission was underway and Tom knew they had the advantage here.

There was once a track across the valley, but this had long disappeared, the army made its own path now, slowly caterpillar crawling its way upward towards the forest. Reaching the treeline, the head of the column pushed through the undergrowth, there they found the remains of the old track, now heavily overgrown. Two swordsmen moved forward and hacked their way through the brambles to make the route more passable. By now the boys were beginning to feel the toll of the journey, cold, damp and carrying the weight of their weapons and bags, they were looking forward to a rest and a warm fire. As they entered the forest they began to feel the safety of cover once more, at that moment an arrow hissed past overhead, and then another.

'Shields! Form line! Archers forward, form line!' Shouted Ackron. Ackron's band of warriors rushed forward to form a line of three ranks covering the head of the column. The first band of archers moved forward to form up behind them. Tulea, the Captain of the first band of archers joined Ackron.

'Lay down some arrows, the passing circle appears to be guarded!' Ackron shouted as she approached. Within seconds the first volley of a hundred arrows was in the air. It was thick with trees and terrible terrain for archery, but Ackron's band of warriors were already advancing on the enemy position and they needed some form of support.

'You three stay close by me!' Shouted Ackron, pointing to Shelaine and the boys. In an instant, all the discomfort, damp and cold vanished, feeling nothing but adrenalin and excitement. Shelaine suspected this and that was why she had raised the question with the Chief, but it was too late for discussion now, as they moved forward behind Ackron and his band of warriors.

Another volley of Thon arrows whipped overhead from behind, rattling through branches, causing leaves and twigs to fall. The archers were moving forward at pace behind Ackron's warriors now. Behind them two columns of swordsmen provided cover, one on each flank with the second column of archers in the middle. The spearmen formed line at the rear, closing the whole unit into a square. The entire army moved as one, with all sides protected as they approached the area where the passing circle was located. It was difficult going, the trees blocked any good line of sight, but moving steadily they slowly made progress.

'Front and centre ranks prepare for assault!' Shouted Ackron. The front and centre ranks of Ackron's war band dropped their shoulder bags and heavy furs.

'Assault and fight through!' Screamed Ackron, and the front two ranks charged forward to assault the position. Still no enemy could be seen as the warriors advanced, no more arrows came their way either. Ackron's warriors came to a standstill just beyond a makeshift shelter, there were provisions and the blackened remains of a small fire pit.

'It was a lookout post, no more than two or three of them I'd say, no sign of them now either.' Advised Edrik as he picked through the remains.

'Those arrows were meant to slow us down in order for them to make their escape.' Akron noted as he scanned around. 'Get the troops reassembled and we'll continue with the mission. Captains gather in!' Each Captain rushed forward to where Ackron stood. 'We just encountered a small lookout party; I suspect they fired their arrows to slow us down in order to escape and report back. Archers gather what arrows you can, then all units come forward and close ranks. We will proceed through the passing circle in column as planned.' The captains acknowledged and went back to their units. 'It seems that you were the only one amongst us who suspected this Shelaine, I'm sorry we didn't consider it more seriously.'

'I suppose it's what I would have done if I were in the

enemy's shoes. Soon the castle will know what we are up to, is it worth tracking down the scouts?' Replied Shelaine.

'I would like to, but I fear our mission is more important, Thon still has plenty warriors to defend itself, so let's make haste to Dornachrov.' Shelaine and the boys gathered round as she pulled out her book and opened the cover. The cross was in the passing circle and the pages were readable again, she ran a finger down the contents page.

'Magellion, Yarromovia, Restilliak, Cregheligan, England, Dornachrov, Esbardach, Undacragov, Elmatoch.' Pausing a moment Shelaine turned to Damien. 'England, isn't that where you two are from?'

'Yes, but I'm not sure mum would appreciate us pitching up with six hundred warriors to feed.' Laughed Damien, Shelaine chuckled and turned to the page for Dornachrov.

The warrior bands gathered; six columns closely packed together. The passing circle was little more than a clearing in the forest as Ackron and his Knights stood to face the warriors. 'Warriors of Thon, listen carefully! Once the passage from this book is read, begin to march through the clearing and don't stop marching until we reach Dornachrov.' Ackron had never travelled with a book before, but the Elder had instructed him on how to bring an army through 'I will lead, Shelaine and the other Knights will enter last, the portal will remain open until the book has passed through.' Ackron paused, observing the apprehension across the faces of his warriors. 'You must pass through before the book, or you will become stranded.' These were important words, Ackron knew that if they encountered trouble, they could end up trapped in hostile lands without the means to return, and this knowledge haunted him.

When all the warriors had reformed into column, Shelaine raised the book, took a deep breath, then began to recite the passage.

'Elders of the book of Cregheligan,
we seek channel to Dornachrov,
through worlds afar,
part the elements,
part time and space,
through the void of existence grant this journey.'

The ground began to vibrate, birds lifted out of their resting places and flew in all directions, the circle began to open, and the army of Thon advanced.

Chapter 16
Strengthening Defences

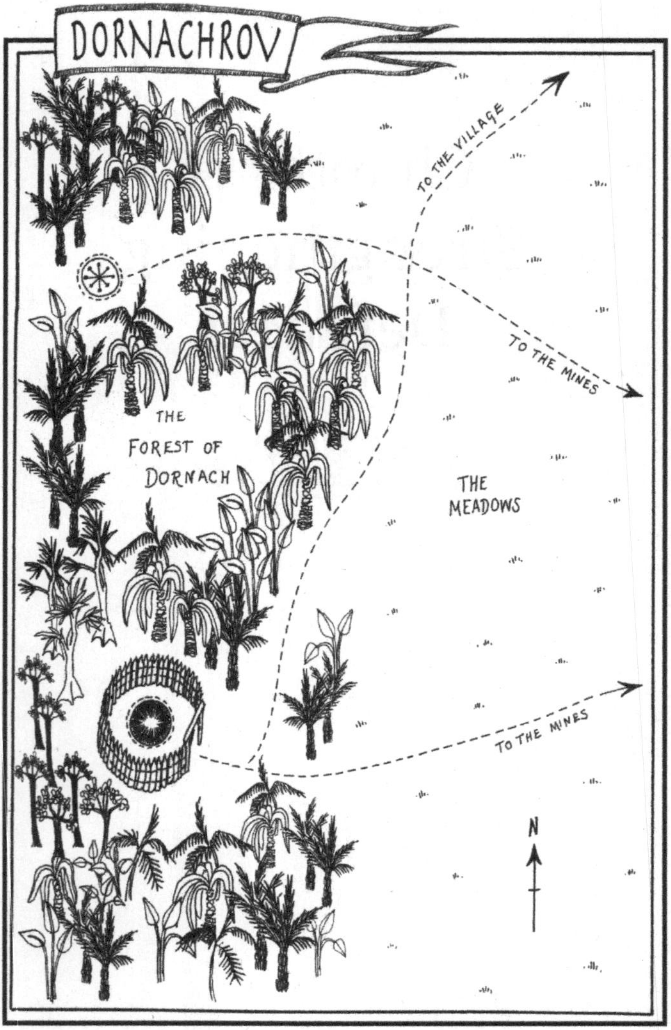
DORNACHROV
TO THE VILLAGE
TO THE MINES
THE FOREST OF DORNACH
THE MEADOWS
TO THE MINES
N

Doon sat on a fallen tree, surrounded by the sandy paleness of freshly cut axe chippings. A Dornach warband, shirtless and breathless rested after felling trees all morning. The Dornachs had been repairing the old fort since the boys left, and much of it was now complete. Its earth mound, now cleared of rotted wooden stakes and made taller, while freshly cut stakes were prepared and set in place. The clearing possessed a strange mystery about it, a serene silence seemed to haunt the place. There was still work to be done, it was never anticipated that this place would ever see use again and so it was left to decay. *Time eats away at the things we build, yet a grudge lasts forever* thought Doon, gazing at a handful of wood chippings. The Dornach warriors rested in the humidity and heaviness of midday, made worse by the pungently scented undergrowth around them. They knew little of what to expect, lethargic and tired, yet devoted to their task nonetheless.

It started with a low and distant humming sound, birds roosting in nearby trees lifted into the air, scattering in all directions, screeching and cawing with fear. The earth around the fort began to vibrate, lethargy morphed into excitement as the unimaginable began to unfold before them.

'On your feet, form line!' Shouted Doon as he stepped forward, spear at the ready, his warriors scrambled into line alongside their leader, spears tilted forward. They looked towards the old fort, and through the entrance of the barricade, the inner space filled with a thick low-lying mist. The earth trembled around them, shaking leaves from trees and rubble from the old barricade walls. As the mist grew thicker, silhouettes slowly began to take form, as the warriors of Thon marched through towards them.

Column after column advanced through the mist

towards Doon and his warband, immediately recognising Tom and Damien, Doon came forward greeting them with a broad smile.

'You made it! Welcome back, welcome!' Called Doon. The Dornach warriors sighed with relief, realising they were facing friendly forces they rested their spears. Line after line of Thon warriors marched through the mist and out of the fort, forming six columns of bear-like figures all ready for combat.

Tom and Damien rushed forward to meet Doon.

'Look at you! New outfits! Now you really look like warriors.' Laughed Doon as the boys greeted him with hugs.

When the last of the warriors came through, Shelaine calmly stepped forward alongside Ackron while the portal closed behind them.

'Doon, this is Ackron, son of the Chief of Thon, and this is Shelaine of Cregheligan.' Announced Tom.

'Welcome to Dornachrov, and thank you for coming to our assistance!' Smiled Doon.

'Once more our forces become one against the Yarromites, and if you hadn't sent these two, I might still be rotting away in Hagleen dungeon. As you can see, they have all been rewarded for their efforts.' Akron took Damien's arm and revealed the Warrior Knight brand of Thon.

Doon smiled with pride. 'I see you have kept busy while away.'

'To be honest, I think the brand was worse than the battle itself.' Added Damien, to which they all laughed.

'We have started to repair defences, and the beginnings of an accommodation site are being prepared a little further into the forest.' Said Doon, indicating with his spear. 'We need to arm your warriors with Ember pearl, that's what the Yarromites will be coming for I suspect, but I imagine you need to rest and eat first, there's food and drink by the fire?' Above the fire pit was a large roasting spit, the smell of wild boar filled the camp as it turned and roasted.

'Thank you' replied Ackron 'Hedoth, get the warriors to rest, we will be moving out again within the hour.' Hedoth acknowledged, Akron then called forward his Captains.

Tulea was a tall woman, with short black braided hair, she wore a simple, light brown leather jerkin, and her left forearm carried the brand of Warrior Knight. Karrell was tall and well built, more akin to a warrior than an archer. She too wore a similar jerkin but with a single braid of blond hair trailing down to the left of her head. The other side was completely shaved and tattooed with an intricate deep blue pattern of weaves and triangular symbols. Both wore a quiver around their waist filled with arrows, a bow slung across the back and a short sword on the waistbelt. Tulea and Karrell each commanded a unit of one-hundred formidable archers, all experts with a bow.

'Captain Tulea, once your archers are fed and rested, prepare them for moving off, you'll be joining me and my warriors for the mines.' Tulea acknowledged. 'Captains Reeval Borgas, Duntan and Karrell, remain here and reinforce the defences around the portal. In addition, a camp is being prepared some distance away on higher ground, send some troops to help with that.' Akron turned to Reeval 'Captain Reeval, you have command here in my absence.'

'Yes Sir!' Replied Reeval.

Akron, Doon, Shelaine and the boys gathered together over roasted meat and goblets of mead. The smoky flavour of the wild boar brought a warming sense of comfort for Tom, barbecues and childhood memories. He sort of wished he was back in that garden, kicking a ball with Damien, or just planning the next trip to the woods. He sat half-listening to the planning going on around him, thinking how different it all was now that it was real. The thought of the farmer and his dog didn't frighten him anymore; he had witnessed death up close and felt the adrenalin of real danger. He now began to realise how close to death he really was.

'Then it seems we are agreed, the Yarromites intend to return?' Asked Doon.

'Oh, without doubt!' Replied Akron. 'They want access to your ember pearl, and the annihilation of the Warriors of Thon.'

'Well, they couldn't finish us last time, and they won't finish us now.' Growled Edrik.

'I'm surprised they haven't come here already.' Muffled Hedoth through a mouthful of roasted meat.

'They must have been as surprised as we were, and just as unprepared I should imagine.' Added Ackron, cutting a slice of meat from the bone. 'The Yarromites don't take uncalculated risks. When they come, they will come in force, and we need to be ready.' Shelaine, Tom and Damien sat in silence, listening to the conversation. 'I've put Reeval in charge here, he's one of the best at laying out defences, we should stand a good chance at holding off any invasion.'

'Ronat is rounding up as many volunteers as he can from the north, but it will take time. We can't be sure when he'll arrive, so we should make a move, head to the mines as soon as we can.' Added Doon.

'Agreed!' Replied Akron. 'Captain Tulea! Prepare the troops to move out.' Tulea acknowledged, within minutes, two-hundred swords and archers had formed up awaiting the order to move.

Tom, Damien and Shelaine joined forces with Doon and his warband, together with Ackron, Hedoth and Edrik.

Ackron turned to Reeval, 'We shall be back before nightfall!' he shouted, then turning to his warriors and archers he gave the command 'Forward!'

Behind him two-hundred warriors of Thon started their march to the ember pearl mines, coiling their way through the forest and down towards the valley floor.

'It will take us around three hours to reach the mines, but we can get refreshment there before the journey back.' Advised Doon as he walked alongside Ackron.

Captain Reeval was tall and broad chested, a well-built warrior, and a respected Commander. He was a good organiser and an excellent tactician, if anyone knew how to setup a defensive position it was Reeval. Calling together the other three Captains, he explained what was required of each. 'Captain Borgas, take your warriors to the accommodation site, you should find a party of Dornachs there, help out however you can.'

'Yes Captain.' Replied Borgas, nodding then turning to muster the one-hundred warriors under his command.

'Captain Duntan, I'd like you to focus your spearmen on the cavalry traps, and the path leading from the portal. There are stakes to be positioned and the left flank is yet to be dug.' Reeval pointed out the area of attention. 'You'll find plenty of tools beyond the rest area.'

Duntan nodded. 'Spears! On your feet! There's digging to be done.' Duntan was a hard-working no-nonsense fellow, he wasted no time with formalities.

'Captain Karrell, you have the pleasure of the archery mound to work on.' Reeval led Karrell to a raised horseshoe mound, east of the defences. 'As you can see, the Dornachs have worked hard on this, but there are plenty more stakes to be dug-in here. I'll leave that task with you.'

'Certainly Captain.' Replied Karrell.

Reeval knew the task of constructing defences would fall to him before they had even arrived, it was this kind of responsibility he thrived on. Much of the repair work had been done to the existing barricades, but the addition of extra trenches and sharpened stakes was required. Cavalry were the greatest threat to Reveal's defences, the warriors of Thon and the Dornachs lacked cavalry, and a well-disciplined Yarromite cavalry troop could scatter defenders in minutes. Cavalry would struggle to hold ground, but they could clear it, and make way for foot soldiers to take and hold it, and this was a very serious threat to the defenders.

The path from the portal had been built up on either side with an earth mound, both mounds running in parallel would act as a corridor forty paces long. Spearmen now worked to add sharpened poles to channel the enemy to where the defenders wanted them, the killing zone. Once the fighting trenches were finished, Reeval's warriors would move on to help the spearmen complete thier task. The whole army worked to support each other.

Several wide cavalry traps were dug at the end of that corridor, ideally these would have been filled with oil or pitch, ready to be ignited, but these supplies were not available, and so the trenches would have to act on their own for now. Reeval had seen what ember pearl could do when ignited, and so he kept this in mind if they were lucky enough to receive a batch of it before the inevitable invasion. Captain Reeval knew it would be a hard fight to defend this area, yet he also knew attacking was always harder than defending.

The afternoon sun broke through a lime-green leafy umbrella, high above the heads of the warriors. It was warm as they worked, building up defences. Weapons, furs and armour had all been shed and stacked close by to make life a little easier, but it was hard work. Reeval encouraged them as he paced about the site inspecting progress, checking for anything that might have been overlooked, he needn't have bothered, his planning was sound, made ever more so by his attention to detail, nothing went unnoticed. Further uphill, deeper into forest, a camp and clearing were built, shelters crafted from nearby trees. This was not a permanent base as yet; it was intended to be nothing more than a comfortable resting place and a place to feed the troops. Ultimately, the six-hundred warriors would be split into three guard shifts, each would rotate every eight hours. Enough shelter for two-hundred warriors to sleep, while two-hundred would guard the portal. The remaining two-hundred would carry out the task of supporting the camp, transporting rations, improving defences or preparing food. They were used to this, it was a standard routine they applied back in Thon, and once the planning was complete, it took little management to see it through.

The march to the Ember pearl mines was a long one, Doon led the way while Tom and Damien described their experience of meeting the warriors of Thon. Doon listened carefully as the boys told their story of the rescue of Ackron from Hagleen castle. Damien described how they were branded Knights of Thon, at least the moments he remembered before passing out. Tom filled in the rest of the story, as their path began to weave its way out of the forest and into a fresh green meadow. Beyond this lay the valley floor, then a track winding its way upwards through the hills of Dornachrov. The track was dry and dusty, seemingly never-ending as the group lumbered on. Each hill crest gave way to the next as the air became somewhat cooler and the vegetation less. Cropped grasses covered the hills as tired footsteps trod the dry dusty path. Occasionally they would stop for a water break or a mouthful of food, and when they did, they began to notice their surroundings in more detail. Scatterings of mountain goats in the distance, heads bowed, slowly, methodically chewing at what greenery they could find. There were few sounds other than the occasional hum of insects, or the rustle of grasses as the warming afternoon breeze swept by.

Continuing on they followed the track until they could see a steeper, craggy hillside in the distance. The hill was speckled with several tunnel entrances, two of which had narrow rail tracks curving out and gently traversing the slope to a large plateau further down. The tracks merged into one before disappearing behind a large wooden palisade, inside were several long buildings all laid out with military precision. The whole site projected an industrial presence in stark contrast to the landscape in which it stood. Black soot trails dusted the landscape like broad charcoal lines on a sketchpad, each highlighting a track or path where ember pearl was being transported.

'It looks like an old coal mine.' Damian noted.

Doon looked around 'What's coal?'

'Well, it's a fossil fuel, we dig it up and burn it for heat or generating electricity. It's less commonly used these days as we have other ways of generating energy.'

'What is electricity?'

'Hmmm, well, it helps do our work for us, and do it

faster I guess, it can generate light and heat, and power machinery.'

'Sounds useful, maybe you could bring some back for us next time you travel home?'

'Haha yes I could try, I few buckets full maybe?'

'That would be great, thank you! You'd need to show us how to use it of course.'

'I'll do my best.' Chuckled Damien as Tom shook his head in bewilderment.

They began to draw closer to the mines, and as they did they were able to make out more detail of the area. Occasionally, a cart would appear from one of the holes like a mouse, pushed out of the mine by two workers then released to roll forward. Momentum carried it towards the workshops as it slowed and disappeared within a small side gate. To the rear of the compound a much steeper track stretched upward, this one had a pully system which was constantly running. A few moments after a cart arrived another would be hauled up the steep track and sent back to an adjacent mine opening to replace it. The only workers visible were the ones who pushed out the carts from the tunnel, and the place appeared to run like clockwork.

Rising up at each corner of the compound stood a tower, tall and square with a lookout in each. On seeing the war band approach, the sound of a horn echoed out and within minutes a troop of warriors filtered out to form a line in front of the gatehouse. At the same time, archers began appearing along the battlements of the palisade walls. The track which Doon and his war band marched along led them straight to the gatehouse.

'Morraine! I'm very impressed, you're awake! What happened, did you wet the bed?'

'Have a little respect for your elders' young man, I recall

bathing you as a child, and it was you who was wetting the bed then!' laughed Morraine as he came forward to hug Doon.

'It's good to see you again my boy, I had word that the old fort defences were to be repaired, but I didn't expect to see you so soon.' Gesturing them inside 'We have all the ember pearl you need, and there's fresh water and rations for your warriors inside. Turic! Show our visitors to the cook house.' Barked Morraine.

'Yes Sergeant!' A voice answered from the ranks as a young warrior ran forward.

Sergeant Morraine was an old warrior, short with a heavy build and as strong as the odour which clung to his battered leather waistcoat. Morraine was one not to be messed with, he could drink, fight and debate, and he did, all night long if he wanted to. Yet he was also a kind-hearted, gentle soul who cared dearly for his nephew Doon.

Ackron's warriors and Tulea's archers followed Turic into the compound to replenish supplies for the journey back, while Doon introduced Ackron to Morraine.

'It's an honour to meet you Ackron son of Egreth, Dornachrov is grateful for your support.' Morraine grabbed Ackron's hand with both of his and shook firmly. Then turned to Tom and Damien. 'I've met you two before! A little less muddy this time thankfully. You have helped Dornachrov a great deal and it isn't the first time, thank you!' Morraine smiled warmly, his rosy cheeks glowed with gratitude as he greeted Tom and Damien, patting them both on the shoulder.

'This is Shelaine of Cregheligan, she, along with these two are now Warrior Knights of Thon.' Announced Ackron proudly. Morraine's eyebrows raised.

'Warrior Knights of Thon, what in the name of the Elders

have you been doing these past few weeks?'

'If it were not for these three, I would not be alive today.' Ackron gazed solemnly at the three of them, as Morraine stood speechless.

'That's a story, I need to hear, but first we have some work to do.' Morraine led them through the gates of the compound and along a broad lane past the processing sheds. The place had a strong smell of grease and timber about it, *like old railway sheds* thought Tom as they walked on between the buildings.

'These are where we process the ore once it arrives from the mine, first we grind it, then we rinse it, and then we add a few more minerals to it before mixing and drying.' Morraine gestured to various wooden buildings along the route, all similar, dark, oily-brown from years of weather beating.

'After drying, the ember pearl is barrelled and stacked here, ready to be made into whatever we need. Arrows, bombs, even firelighters. We then store the finished products in those warehouses, and that is where your consignment is.' Pointing to a row of much larger wooden buildings standing apart from the main compound. From his waistcoat pocket Morraine pulled out a large iron keyring as they approached the first building, he selected a key and pushing it into an iron lock he turned. The door moaned a creak as he pulled hard on it, reaching inside, Doon lifted a latch and pulled on the other door. The weather-gnarled wooden doors slowly opened with the gaping yawn of a sleepy giant as the rest of the group stood in awe. Row upon row of wooden hand carts disappeared into the darkness of the warehouse, there were no lamps, it was too dangerous to introduce a naked flame here. Instead, small shutters high up on the walls offered a dimly lit view of the interior.

'All the carts are identical, but the contents vary. Round barrels are for the archers and rectangular crates contain bombs. Each cart has two carrying poles alongside, four people per cart. Carry them carefully and don't drop them, the contents are designed to explode on impact!' Morraine continued to deliver his safety brief as he led the group deeper into the darkness.

'There are shutters on the sides of the building, you can lift some of these for better light, but no lamps or torches in here!'

Shelaine and the boys looked around, there were too many to count. 'Fifty carts for the archers and fifty carts of bombs, that's what we are taking back with us today. Going forward I shall send a smaller war band each day to build up supplies near the village.' Doon added. Morraine nodded as he took a pole and began to lift one of the side shutters to let in more light. This was just one of several warehouses, each filled with carts and ember pearl containers. A heavy oily, greasy odour hung about the place, it seemed to cling to everything, the walls, the carts and the floor. It was strong and overpowering, but not unpleasant, reminding Damien of a visit to a steam train museum many years ago with his grandfather.

'Don't get them wet! We grease or wax everything to keep the damp out, the canvas covers, the carts, the boxes, everything! The charges are all wrapped in waxed paper too.' Advised Morraine.

'Now it makes sense!' Thought Damien, out loud.

'What?' Enquired Tom.

'The smell, the grease is for waterproofing, it's just like gunpowder, you have to keep it dry or it doesn't work.'

'Oh right.' Replied Tom, still a little unsure of the conversation trail.

Ackron turned to Doon 'I should get the troops organised;

it's going to be a slow march back.'

'Agreed, we can't rush the transportation of this.'

Doon turned to Tom and Damien.

'Let me show you what we're taking back.'

Approaching one of the carts he untied a rope and pulled back the waxed canvas that covered it. Beneath the canvas there were twelve small oak barrels stacked in a single layer with the lids uppermost. Doon lifted one out and placed it on top of the others. Taking a knife from his belt, he carefully prized off the lid. Inside the barrel was a layer of coiled twine on top of some straw packing. Removing the straw revealed the tops of the round tubes beneath, packed like fine pencils. Doon slid one out, it was almost exactly like a pencil in shape and length.

'This is what is attached to your arrows Damien, each one whipped to the arrow shaft with the twine, when the arrow strikes home, the charge explodes. Pass me a plain arrow.' Damien selected an arrow from his quiver and handed it to Doon. Taking a short length of twine, Doon made a loop at one end, holding it along the arrow and the charge, he placed a thumb over it. He then started to wind the lose length of the twine firmly around both the arrow, the charge and the open end of the loop. He continued until reaching the end where the loop was poking out, he threaded the lose end of the twine through the loop then pulled on the opposite end of the twine to draw it tight against itself. He repeated the process at both ends of the charge so that it was firmly fixed to the arrow shaft.

'This will need to be done for all the charges. We have twenty-five carts; each cart contains twelve barrels and each barrel contains fifty charges. As soon as we get back, we will need to distribute these to the archers and show them what I've just shown you. I want every archer to carry twenty-four arrows, we will keep the remainder in reserve, at both the camp and the village.' Doon handed the arrow back to Damien who slid it carefully into his quiver.

Doon then walked over to another cart on the opposite row. 'These are the bombs; we have twenty-five carts of these.' Again, he untied the rope and threw back the canvas. Beneath the oily cloth were six rectangular crates, placing the tip of his blade under the lid of one he prized it open, inside was what looked like a long coil of thick string with red marks at equal intervals along it. The string was placed on a straw bed covering twelve dark brown, egg-shaped bombs, each about the size of a lemon and protected by straw. 'This is the fuse, each mark indicates 5 seconds, you cut the fuse to the length of time you need, then insert one end into the bomb.' He took out one of the bombs and handed it to Damien, it wasn't heavy, a cold clay case with a wooden plug poking out at one end. 'To prime the bomb we remove the plug, insert one end of the fuse as far as it will go, then push the plug back to fix it into place.' Doon cut off 15 second worth of fuse and handed it to Tom. Tom's hands were clammy with sweat as he took the fuse and carefully pulled out the plug, inserting one end of the fuse into the bomb he pushed the plug back tight. 'Perfect! Now, to ignite the fuse you can either place it against a rock then strike it hard with another, or ignite it with a flame. Either works just fine, or if you are really desperate you can just throw it without a fuse, the impact will usually set off the bomb, but not always, it depends what it lands on.' Tom handed the bomb back to Doon who removed the fuse and placed both back in the box. 'You need to keep a good distance from these, if you are setting a trap the effect and blast area increases with the number of bombs used, so be very careful, you could easily kill yourself in the process.'

Tom wiped his palms 'I think I'm happy to leave that to the experts, or Damian for that matter.' Tom grinned.

'Of course, but it's important that you know about these to avoid any mistakes. One bomb for each warrior and some in reserve for Captain Reeval.' Replied Doon.

At that point Akron arrived with the warbands following behind. 'Here, brought you some food and water, you haven't eaten yet.' Akron handed out small packs to the four of them. 'Hand carts! This is going to be a slow march back. We should probably get moving soon, Captain Tulea, split the warbands into groups of four and have them take a cart each!' Tulea acknowledged and began directing the troops.

'The carts aren't heavy, but we do need to go easy moving them around, and we need to keep the contents dry.' Shouted Doon as the troops began to slide the carrying poles into slots on either side of the carts. Doon then turned to Morraine 'Thank you for preparing this first batch. We are going to need much more, but this should go some way towards strengthening our existing defences.'

'At the rate this lot are working; we can have the same amount ready in five or six days, so don't worry lad, there's plenty more for you when you need it. Travel easy with them and look after yourselves!' Morraine turned and with a heavy sigh made his way back towards the guardhouse. He had been preparing for this moment for a long time, hoping silently that it would never come, and so he felt no pleasure in knowing his work had found its purpose at last.

'Archers! Warriors! Prepare to lift, lift! In single file, lead off!' Doon led the army out of the building and along the track, as they passed through the gatehouse, he looked up to see Morraine watching from the palisade above.

Shelaine walked alongside one of the carts, then pushed

back the oilskin. Easing off a lid with her knife she took three charges and some twine. 'If we are not carrying then we might as well start whipping these onto arrows.' Drawing two arrows from Damien's quiver she passed one to Tom.

'Good thinking!' Replied Tom as he started to loop the twine and began whipping the charge into place. After an hour or so, they had emptied several barrels taking regular arrows from the archers and redistributing explosive ones. Even Doon, Ackron, Edrik and Hedoth had joined in the task. Shelaine was excellent at organisation and forward thinking, and she knew the importance of what it was they were preparing for.

The route back from the mines was slow, each cart had a carrier at every corner, and at times they would halt in order to swap positions, relieving tired arms.

'I'm managing one arrow a minute now!' Smiled Tom.

'I always knew you'd do well in life. Guess that's what being born into wealth does.' Mocked Damien, as the others laughed along.

'Wealth? I'm from working class stock just like you!' Responded Tom.

'Oh, you say that, but I know different.'

'What are you talking about? Prove it!' Replied Tom, by now the group around them were beginning to chuckle as the banter continued.

'Sandwiches! I rest my case your honour.'

'Sandwiches? Did someone fill your water bottle with mead or something?' Tom's face screwed up in confusion.

'Listen and learn my boy. It's all down to the way a parent makes sandwiches. Your's cut them into triangles, and therefore you are middleclass. If they cut them into triangles and removed the crust, you would be upper class.

If they cut them into rectangles, you would be working class, and if they didn't cut them at all, you would be poor.' Offered Damien confidently as the others began to laugh at the way these two mocked each other.

'You're an idiot, and if I weren't carrying enough explosives to redesign this hillside, I'd kick your working-class ass, boy!' The pair of them laughed together, it felt like old times, back in Hinckleford, when banter and boyhood were the most import things in life. Something heavier took that place now, something more important than who could run faster, who could cycle fastest down the hill, or get the most bounces from a skimmed stone on a pond. There was a sense of loss in growing up so soon.

On reaching the final hill crest, the valley floor came into view below, beyond that, stood the forest, it was a welcome sight. Ackron halted the line and ordered the troops to rest. They were tired, one cart had already been emptied of arrows and left by the side of the track. Those no longer carrying carts had joined in the task of whipping charges to arrows, and they were making good progress overall.

It was late-afternoon, a light breeze swayed meadow grass like a Mexican wave through the valley ahead of them. Tom loosened the cork stopper from his water bottle and looked inside, it was almost empty, but not much further to go. He took a mouthful, leaving the same amount in the bottle for the rest of the journey, at least in the forest it would be cooler.

'Hey did you see that? There it is again! Like a flashing light in the forest.' Damien was pointing and staring at a patch of trees about half way up the hillside. 'There it goes again, all swimmy and blurry.'

'Pick up the carts, pick up the carts!' Screamed Doon. 'It's the portal, it's opening!'

Chapter 17
Invasion

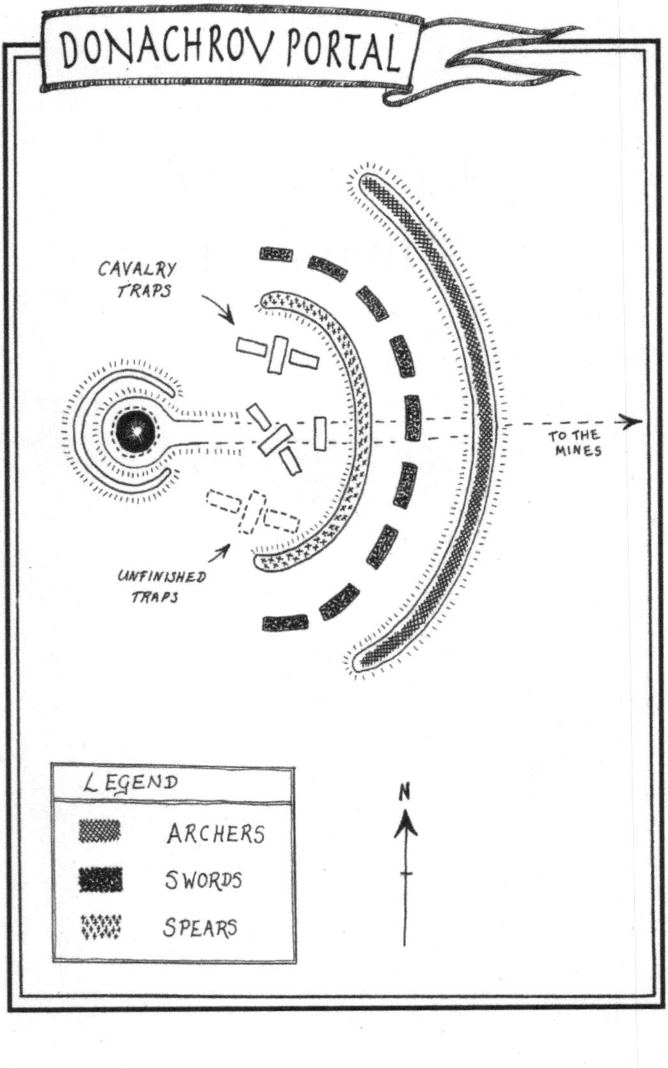
DONACHROV PORTAL
CAVALRY TRAPS
UNFINISHED TRAPS
TO THE MINES
LEGEND
ARCHERS
SWORDS
SPEARS
N

Conrach slouched back in his saddle, holding the book in one hand and slowly turning the pages with the other. 'Dornachrov!' he began to read aloud from the page, beside him stood two-hundred archers in four ranks of fifty, bows at the ready. Alongside, two-hundred mounted lancers stood in column formation ready to advance. Horses bowed and raised their heads against leather reins as steam puffed from flared nostrils. The air filled with the smell of horse and leather, riders seated firmly with reins resting over white, leather gloved hands, awaiting the order to advance. It was early, a fresh cold mist hung close to the ground, the cavalry looked superb, brightly polished breast plates and helmets adorned with crimson red plumes, lances pointing skyward. Each horseman carried a lance, a long, white Ash pole tipped with a sharpened steel point, the opposite end fitted with a polished steel cap. They stood waiting, side by side extending back into the mist of the forest, as Conrach's words began to awaken the portal. 'Commander Burwell, it is time to conquer Dornachrov!'

A grandiose statement and Burwell knew it, they were only here for the Ember pearl on this occasion, but he allowed Conrach his moment. Burwell's horse stood several paces to the left of his archers, behind the archers stood the main body of foot soldiers, four-hundred swordsmen ready to advance. To Burwell's left were his bugler, staff officers and Conrach. He looked down the line, feeling both pride and also hint of despair that his magnificent troops were about to enter battle, knowing many would not return. Then taking a slow deep breath, he gave the command. 'Archers, Notch!' Each took an arrow from its quiver and carefully placed the notch against the bowstring. 'Draw!' Two-hundred archers raised their bows to forty-five degrees and drew back. 'Loose!' The sky turned grey, filled with a cloud of Ash and feather, another hail of arrows followed, disappearing through the portal.

Captain Reeval inspected the defences, every element, from the archery mound, past the warrior fighting trenches, through the spear trenches to the cavalry traps. The traps were made up of deep randomly positioned pits, now lined with sharpened wooden stakes, the right of flank was complete, the centre was still under construction, but the left flank had only been marked out with piles of stakes beside them. A work-party of spearmen hacked and shovelled the ground, positioning a fresh row of stakes. They focused their attention on the central obstacles set out to hinder the approach of cavalry. Further back, groups of swordsmen and archers fortified the defensive mound to the rear. Reeval walked over to the left of field where three pits had been marked out ready to dig. 'We need these finished before nightfall!' Reeval called out to one of his Corporals. At that moment a rush of air swirled around him, shimmers and flashes of light burst from the direction of the portal forty paces down the track, and the sky turned grey.

'Stand to arms! Stand to arms!' Reeval shouted to a boy whose job it was to sound the alarm, the boy raised a curled bull horn to his lips, filled his lungs then was sharply jolted backward to the ground. Reeval leapt over a pile of stakes that separated them and crouched beside him, taking the horn, he blew hard. The forest echoed with a haunting shrill, carrying beneath the leafy canopy to alert the remaining warriors. The pale shaft of an arrow projecting skyward from the boy's shoulder dithered as he writhed in pain. He panicked, franticly trying to kick backwards to the safety of a nearby trench. Reeval scrambled to his knees as an arrow lanced into the soft earth beside him, grabbing the boy's collar he ran, arrows punched into the earth around them as more streaks of white feather flashed by. Jumping down into one of the unfinished trenches Reeval pulled the boy in propping him up against the trench wall. 'It's alright lad, you'll survive this, but stay here and keep covered.' Reeval took the horn and blew again, he looked over the trench wall to get a better view of the situation. Arrows continued raining down ahead of him, he could see three spearmen dead beside an unfinished trench, to the right of them another was calling out in pain. Reeval heaved himself out of his position and ran towards the warrior, the ground was now splintered with arrow shafts and feathers, both the spearman's legs had been hit as he tried to pull himself to safety. Reeval grabbed an arm and dragged him through the prongs of arrows back towards the spear trench. Further back the arrows grew less, the horseshoe curve of the spear trench was almost out of range of the enemy archers. Reeval dropped down into the trench where he had left the boy, pulling the spearman in behind. 'Stay here, I'll send help.' Clambering out again as another arrow struck the side wall of the trench beside him, Reeval ran back towards the fighting trenches. 'I have two wounded in that trench, get them back to camp!' He shouted as he approached a group of spearmen who were now advancing to take up positions. The remainder of the guard were forming up, one-hundred archers spread out along the mound, in front of them the warriors prepared themselves in their fighting trenches. Running up towards the archers Reeval called out for Captain Karrell.

'Over here Captain Reeval!'

'I need you to allocate twenty archers to the spear trench,

ten on either flank to act as skirmishers. Then prepare the remainder to repel an assault.' Karrell acknowledged.

Reeval knew the initial barrage of arrows was just a precursor to assault, what he didn't know was how that assault might take form, foot soldiers or mounted, he had to prepare for both and with limited resources.

Captain Karrell sent forward twenty archers, ten to either flank of the spear trench. Their role would be to take opportunistic shots at any target they could in order to slow and disrupt the assault. Twenty archers weren't many, but they could certainly help disrupt an organised attack on the spear trenches. The remaining archers spread out along the horseshoe shaped mound; they stuck arrows into the soft earth beside them to make for faster notching. Behind the mound several younger trainees' unlaced large round leather rolls filled with neatly packed arrows, inside each roll was a small leather pouch to hold extra bowstrings. Everything was packed meticulously to keep out moisture; this was essential, as a damp bowstring wouldn't perform as well as a dry one. The trainees always went into battle with the archers, their work was mostly to assist in keeping the archers supplied, but they too could handle a bow, and knew how to fight if it came to it.

Captain Reeval walked forward to the fighting trenches to join his warriors, this is where the main focus of battle would likely be. The trenches only acted as shelter from arrows and charging cavalry, the actual fighting would take place forward of these. By using these trenches for protection, it also gave Thon's archers a clear view of any approaching threat, and the opportunity to hinder that threat without hitting their own warriors.

The defenders used horns to issue commands, spears engage, spears take cover, warriors engage, warriors take cover, archers engage, archers take cover. It was a simple, yet effective means to organise and control the actions of troops on the battlefield, and everyone knew exactly what to listen out for. Three different pitches indicated which body of troops should respond, and two simple notes, slow long blows to take cover, and short rapid blows to engage. The individual captains would manage the actual units, but horns were a means to manage the readiness of the whole army. There was one other pitch which was deeper and louder than the rest, this was used to sound the general alarm, and it was this that Reeval sounded after the boy was wounded.

Reeval would have preferred to remain with his warriors today, this was his usual fighting position, but from here he could not control the flow of battle. He had to be further back on the archer's mound with a good field of view. He reassured and encouraged his warriors walking down the line of trenches, and then reluctantly made his way back towards the archers.

The arrows lessened to a slow, sporadic shower, a clear indicator to Reeval the next stage of the attack was about to begin. He raised the horn to his lips; covered the first of three holes along the top of the horn then blew. Three long deep tones echoed out into the forest, hearing this the spearmen took cover into their trenches. He covered the first two holes on the horn and blew three long tones again, this time the swordsmen took cover, then finally Reeval covered the first hole and blew three short bursts, the archers who were not already on the mound clambered up, formed line along the top of the mound and waited with bows in hand.

The arrows stopped, looking from the mound towards the portal, the clearing was speckled with tall feather capped stalks protruding from the ground. They had concentrated around the cavalry traps where three dead spearmen lay. The arrows hadn't fully reached the curved spear trench, and the warrior fighting trenches were too far out of range for the Yarromite archers.

Reeval watched the flickering and shimmering lights ahead, he'd never properly looked at the portal until now, in all the chaos he was focused on organising and preparing for the assault, but now he could fully appreciate the magnificence. Pure magic, mysterious ghostly shimmers of light reaching out, snatching at the air then disappearing back into itself, almost liquid in its appearance. The feint, deep humming, rising and falling in the distance like a simmering cooking pot. These were now the only sounds, no birds, no wildlife, just the humming and groaning, then a rumble, distant at first, becoming louder. Reeval looked over at Karrell.

'Captain Karrell, ready your archers!'

Karrell nodded 'Archers, notch!' Her command was loud and fearsome, even the archers in the spear trenches heard it and responded, whether it be fear or force of habit, they were ready. Karrell waited, her bright aquamarine blue eyes wide and alert, scanning for the first shape to emerge. Timing had to be precise, if her archers were to draw too soon the long wait would cause their aim to falter and the first barrage would be less effective. She watched and waited, and then they came. The silver pinpricks of spear tips burst through the watery mists of the portal, charging down the track towards them. 'Draw!' The archers on the mound stretched back their bowstrings to their chins 'Loose!' and the sky whistled with the whirl of feathers in a fast-moving cloud towards the lancers. They notched, drew back again and released a second cloud of arrows just as the first struck home. The first two charging horses fell forward to the ground, riders tumbling over them and crushed beneath. Momentum carried the next few horses forward one of which reared up throwing back it's rider to the ground. Arrows struck hard into leather saddles, horses and lancers as they pounded through and along the track, swerving and slowing to get over the fallen. Reeval watched as the lancers charged through toward the traps, several horses had unseated their riders and were now bolting off in random directions to avoid the chaos. The first few horses reached the traps, one stumbled and fell in on top of its rider, another horse rode over and pounded towards the spear trenches. Reeval sounded the horn for the spearmen to defend, while the skirmishing archers began to loose their arrows causing even more chaos for the attackers.

Once clear of the track, the lancers began to fan out, many of them struck by arrows as they funnelled out and into the wider space. There wasn't enough open ground for them to properly form up, as they frantically fought and rode over whatever stood in their path to break free of the carnage. A gradual flow of lancers continued to break free from the track as more streamed through the portal, traps began to swallow horses and riders as they spilled out and off the track. And as they did, they began to realise that the defences were weaker on the right of their right flank.

This was what Reeval feared most, if enough of the lancers could take advantage of that weakness, then they could form up and outflank the archers. Captain Karrell watched as her archers sent sporadic swarms of arrows towards the advancing cavalry. Noticing how the lancers were moving like a wave towards the left of field Karrell instructed the archers to the right of the mound to peel off and form a defensive position to the rear left of the mound. At the same time, Reeval sounded the horn for the swordsmen to attack.

Ackron could hear the feint echo of the horn and knew that Reeval would need help fast. 'Stash the crates by the side of the track! Captain Tulia, take your archers and whatever charges you have ready then head to the portal now as fast as you can. I want sixty warriors to come with me, grab a handful of bombs each and fuse them with five second fuses on the way!'.

Tom and Damien knew it wasn't looking good; they had been caught out before the defences were ready. Shelaine grabbed four bombs and quickly cutting fuses she inserted them into the bombs, Tom did the same while Damien already had a quiver full of charged arrows. The three of them set off with the archers and a ragtag of warriors following behind, clumsily fusing bombs. Doon instructed the remaining forty warriors to disperse the crates amongst the tall grasses off the track and to hide amongst them as best they could. It was important that these supplies did not fall into enemy hands, and these men would act as a rear guard.

Conrach smiled as Burwell looked over to Calder, his Sergeant of Horse, he then gave the order for his foot soldiers to advance. From their position on the other side of the portal they had no idea of what was going on in Dornachrov. No sound could pass back to them, no vision of progress or failure, just a sense of timing and blind faith that they would succeed in their mission. And so they marched, three ranks of foot soldiers began to emerge into a scene of carnage, horses lay dead along the track, riders pricked with arrows both dead and dying. In the distance, the last of the remaining lancers could be seen peeling off to the right, in order to form line ready to charge. At the sight of the foot soldiers Captain Karrell ordered half of her archers to concentrate their aim on the track again. Shards of Ash whistled through the air towards Calder as he ordered his foot soldiers to draw swords and charge. Hoping for a better fate than that of the lancers around him. At the mouth of the track Sergeant Calder ordered his troops to flank off to his left, he did not wish to become entangled in a cavalry charge. The first unit of foot soldiers pressed on to their left in order to outflank the defending spearmen. On the far right of the defences, the lancers began their charge headlong into the archers from the side and rear of the mound. The Warriors in the centre of field had, until now, remained relatively free from the encounter, but that was about to change. Reeval ordered the spearmen to move in support of the archers, leaving their trenches they rushed to the defence and quickly formed line at the base of the archer's mound, putting themselves between the archers and the cavalry. He then instructed his warriors to do the same in order to cover the archer's right flank. Reeval's force was heavily outnumbered, as the foot soldiers continued to advance through the portal. Lines upon lines, black tunics and silver braid adorned the invaders as they drew swords and advanced to their fighting positions. Slowly and intimidatingly, they formed three ranks behind the first unit.

'Warriors of Thon hold your ground!' Ordered Reeval, by now the archers' mound had become the final defensive position, cavalry engaging spearmen on the left of flank and swords clashing to the right. Thon archers loosed arrows at every opportunistic target they could, as the

Yarromite foot soldiers advanced, they were no match for Thon, but there were many more of them. The last of the foot soldiers emerged from the portal as arrows continued to rain down on them, and then came the archers. Hordes of Yarromite archers poured through, rushing forward like a rabble they collected arrows from the ground as they ran, behind them, Conrach and Burwell rode together into the horror they had created.

Tulea's archers reached the treeline first and pushed on into the forest. 'Archers form line!' she ordered as they moved uphill towards the site of the portal. In the distance they could hear the horses and clashing of steel, but it was all too deep into the forest to see from this point. It had turned from a well-planned and executed mission, to a disorganised and desperate attempt to regain some control. They didn't know what they were up against, nor where they were up against it, they would need to think on their feet. Shelaine reached the treeline with Tom and Damien close behind. Ackron and his warriors were further back due to the weight of equipment they carried, and Doon further back still.

'Commander Burwell, we need not concern ourselves with a victory here, our mission is to reach the mines!' Conrach shouted, as his horse cantered along the churned-up path, weaving through corpses and wounded. The pair reached the end of the track as Burwell ordered his foot soldiers to disengage and pull back into the forest. The archers pulled back too providing cover for the withdrawal, at the same time stuffing retrieved arrows back into quivers at every opportunity. The lancers, in their attempt to dislodge the archers from the mound were held off by the spearmen. They began to swing around to the rear of the mound for a second attempt. Seeing this, Burwell ordered his bugler to signal the lancers back, in support of the foot soldiers' withdrawal, this would help prevent any counter attack by Thon.

Reeval paced along the top of the mound ensuring his forces were well distributed to withstand a second assault. Keeping an eye on the withdrawing Yarromites as they slowly disappeared into the forest. Reeval expected another assault, and made ready for it, but it never came, and so he instructed the spearmen to check for wounded while the remaining force watched for movement. The field of battle prickled with arrows, dead and wounded of both armies covered the ground, from the portal to the archer's mound.

'Captain Reeval!' A shout echoed from the trees to the rear of the mound, it was Tulea, panting and sweating as she ran towards them with her archers spread out either side. Behind them a trail of others approached, Shelaine, Tom and Damien amongst them.

Chapter 18
Cat and Mouse

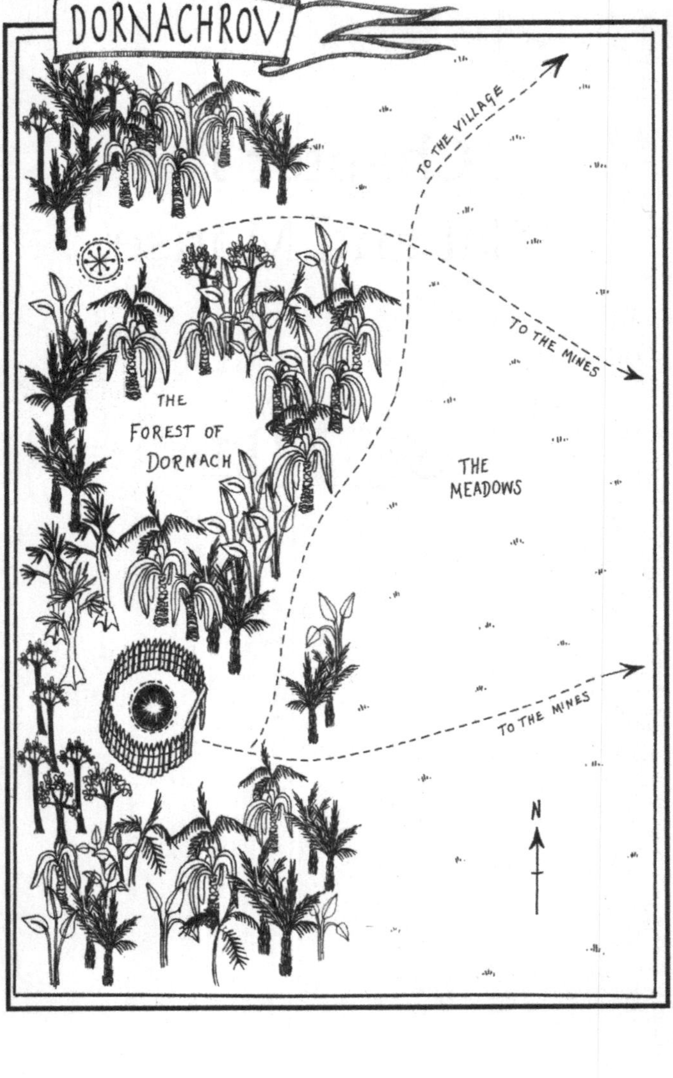
DORNACHROV
TO THE VILLAGE
TO THE MINES
THE FOREST OF DORNACH
THE MEADOWS
TO THE MINES
N

Akron paced as he listened to Reeval describe the events, the others sat around trying to take it all in. 'They could have easily wiped us out, we were heavily outnumbered, yet they didn't, instead they withdrew into the forest to the North.'

'It sounds like they wanted to save their forces for a more important encounter.' Added Akron.

'The mines, they want the ember pearl.' Doon stood up and turned to look in the direction of the ember pearl mines. 'They'll need all the forces they can muster to take as much as possible back to Yarromovia. With that, they can invade any land they choose with greater ease. I was wrong to think they wanted to conquer Dornachrov, at this stage they need to improve their firepower, and strengthen their armies.'

'Then we have to stop them.' Akron turned to Captain Reeval 'Complete the defences here, we can't risk letting any more of them through. I will leave you with a supply of bombs.' Akron paused while looking around 'We will head back to the mines, but I need to take Captain Karrell and her archers with me.'

'Yes Sir!' Acknowledged Reeval.

Wiping the sweat from his forehead Doon looked across the battlefield 'I'll Send word to Ronat, inform him and the Elder of the situation.' His voice low and sombre. 'We are going to need them to send reserves to guard the passing circle. If we can cut off the Yarromites there, we might even be able to take their book from them.' Doon turned to Reeval 'Do you know how many we lost?'

'I'd say around fifty, mostly spears and swordsmen. They lost around forty lancers and almost a hundred soldiers, but there must have been close to a thousand of them.' Reeval glanced over to the portal, it was calm and still, hard to imagine what had just happened, and with such little warning.

'Then we need to move, replenish water and supplies quickly, we must get back to the mines!' Ordered Ackron, Tulea and Karrell acknowledged then stirred their units to replenish supplies and assemble into formation for the march back to the mines.

Doon shouted over to his war band 'I need two volunteers!' Canrick and Tervil, two young Dornach warriors stepped forward. 'Get word to Ronat back at the village. Inform him of the situation here and tell him we need reserves to cut off the Yarromites at the passing circle.' The two young volunteers acknowledged the order, picked up their kit then set off in the direction of the village.

Canrick and Tervil leapt and dashed through the forest, branches scratching and grabbing as they ran. The light was starting to fade, becoming harder to make out the track ahead of them. Twigs scraped on leather, ferns brushed against them, as the earthy scent of nighttime rose to fill the air. They would have preferred to stand and fight with their companions, but they knew it was important to inform Ronat. If he could move his warriors to the passing circle in time, the Yarromites could be stopped. They sprang through the darkness like deer, focused only on where the next foot might land.

By the time they reached the edge of the forest the cold crispness of evening had closed in. Pausing for breath they looked out across the meadows before them, a delicate mist hung over the lower part of the valley. They could follow the treeline, a safer yet slower option, or they could cut directly across the valley. The grass, tall, still and ghostly stood before them, they broke cover and ran. Waist high, the meadow grass rippled as the two messengers ran down towards the mist. Approaching the base of the valley, pockets of mist swirled around, enveloping them from the chest down. Cotton clouds of crisp dampness embraced them as they ran, together with the rhythmical sound of hooves, distant, yet growing stronger.

The sun ebbed as the heat of the day cooled. Tree shadows grew tall where clearings offered space to stretch, Conrach's army marched toward the Passing place. Conrach leaned over his saddle to speak with Burwell 'We must secure the passing place first, and leave a force in position ready to assist the raiding party on their return. I'm sure the Dornachs know by now what our plan is, but they won't know how we intend to execute it.'

Burwell sniggered 'You've thought of everything I see; did you notice the warriors of Thon had joined them?'

'Yes, I did, but that's of no concern to us now. Once we arrive at the passing place our lancers will need to ditch their armour plate and any heavy equipment, they don't even need their lances.' A look of confusion crossed Burwell's face as Conrach continued. 'We will take all the horses, but swap fifty lancers for archers, the archers will act as a raiding party when we arrive at the mines. We take as much ember pearl as we can carry in saddlebags and backpacks, before rejoining the main force at the passing circle.' Burwell nodded, still processing the detail.

Conrach had spent the past few weeks planning this raid, he had not anticipated the Warriors of Thon, but he would not allow this to scupper those plans. Conrach was confident it would succeed, yet such a strong defence at the portal meant he had less resources to transport ember pearl back to Yarromovia, and he knew he could not afford to lose more horses.

It was getting dark as the Yarromites approached the

site of the passing circle. The moon cast its silvered glaze across the forest canopy, ghostly pillars of moonlight broke through, guiding them forward. There was just enough light to find one's way through the sombre shadows of tree trunks and into the clearing. *Silence could drive a person to madness here* thought Burwell as he stepped down from his horse.

'Sergeant Calder!'

'Sir!'

'Have the foot soldiers provide all round defence and have the lancers shed armour and weapons, and I want fifty archers to mount fifty horses, mount the remainder with unarmed lancers. We shall be moving out shortly.' Ordered Burwell.

'Yes Sir!' Calder organised the units without question. The foot soldiers took up low-lying defensive positions all around the passing circle. The lancers ditched all heavy gear, helmets, breastplate and lances, to which there was some resentment, but nonetheless they followed orders. Fifty lancers stepped down from their mounts to help fifty archers mount up. This was a very unusual tactic, but these were unusual times, not one of them could have imagined they would ever be in this situation.

After Burwell had finished organising the troops he walked his horse to the centre of the circle where Conrach was resting. 'We have one hundred and forty-eight horses ready to move out, we lost fifty-two at the portal. The remaining force is providing all round defence of the passing circle for when we return, just as you requested.'

'Good, we should move out now.' Replied Conrach. By now the map was virtually unreadable in moonlight, but Conrach had studied it so many times it didn't matter. Every track and turn were held like a picture in his mind, the forest was the only obstacle, but as long as he went downhill, he would be able to exit and find his bearings from there, maybe two hours journey on horseback he guessed.

'Move off, pass it down the line.' Heaving himself up into the saddle Burwell nudged his horse forward, and the line of cavalry began to snake its way downhill and through the forest.

It was slow, but steady, a cool dampness hung heavy and crisp the further down the valley they went. Hoof after hoof, hardly making a sound through the soft undergrowth. Foaming mouths and steaming nostrils, tail to nose they walked on. Using his peripheral vision Conrach led the way, glancing slightly left and right of the direction he travelled in order to make out the route. His horse seemed to manage just as well if not better, naturally weaving left and right to avoid unrecognisable obstacles in its path. Then in the distance, the silver clouded mist of the valley came into view, almost as clear as daylight in comparison to the blackness of the forest.

Conrach's horse stepped into the open meadow, a delicate mist hung across the shallow dip of grassland, like a mercury pool it held the silvered moonlight ahead of them. In the distance, across the valley, a hillside gently sloping upward and out of the mist. Conrach moved them on a little faster, then he noticed something, movement, crossing right to left through the valley. 'Commander, we have company!' Pointing towards the mist covered valley Conrach indicated to Burwell. Spurs struck home and Burwell's horse jolted forward. Silence broken by the rumbling gallop of a single horse in the moonlight. The hilt of Burwell's sabre felt cold yet comforting as he reached over and drew it from its scabbard. A flash of moonlight glanced off the blade as it slashed forward, a satisfying warmth splashed across the back of his hand as the sabre came down and struck home hard. Turning his horse for a second pass he charged and slashed again. Consumed by the damp mists of the valley the two silhouettes were gone. A wavering column of steam lifted from the place where they fell, as Burwell rejoined the head of the troop.

Cantering through swirling mists they pushed on through the valley. Steam from nostrils bellowed out to mix with the damp air as hooves thumped, hypnotic in rhythm. Burwell wiped the blood from his sabre, carefully returning it to its scabbard.

Shelaine walked beside Tom and Damien; the moon cast its platinum patina over the track ahead. Ackron called out in a low voice for his warriors as they approached the area where the rear guard had been left. 'Over here! Bring in the crates!' Called one warrior to the others.

Gradually the rear guard began to emerge from the darkness, they had used their time wisely, attaching the remaining charges to arrow shafts. 'Excellent work, distribute these to the archers, and the remaining bombs to everyone else.' Akron instructed, taking a handful of arrows and passing them to Damien. 'We are heading back to the mines in order to fend off an assault. Leave the empty crates here and join our ranks.'

Three ranks of warriors ground on along the gravel track, it was slow, and those who had already made the whole journey were exhausted. 'Do you think we can make it in time? The Yarromites have horses.' Tom whispered to Shelaine.

'We may be lucky, if they took time to rest then we could get there before them, but if I were them I would have moved as fast as I could to reach those mines.' Replied Shelaine.

Damien nodded as he fought against the pain of blisters. Damp sweat from the heat of the day had soaked through his shirt, now cold and wet. All he could think of right now was a hot bath followed by a warm bed. He cast his thoughts back to that cosy hut in Thon, with the fire in the open hearth that burned all night, while he curled beneath the warm furs on his bed. Strange that these memories were now more prominent than those of his bedroom back in Hinckleford. His life here was intense, one adventure after another with hardly a moment's rest, and right now he was beginning to feel it.

Conrach halted the cavalry column, raising a curved, stubby finger he pointed to a feint amber glow in the distance. 'There, see it, that's the gatehouse!' He was almost shaking with excitement. 'We take that first, open the gate and then allow the main body of troops to walk their horses straight in. We find the stores and take all that we can carry, pack everything into saddlebags and pouches then leave as silently as we arrived.'

'I can't guarantee the horses won't startle and bring attention upon us, but we will just have to chance it.' Replied Burwell, Conrach tapped his heels into his horse, if he heard Burwell, he didn't acknowledge.

The mounted troops followed suit as the feint orange glow grew larger. At first, it looked like a lantern, but as they drew closer, they could see it was the top of a brasier, perched upon the palisade wall of the gatehouse. Conrach halted the troop a short distance away so as not to alert the guards, Burwell selected six archers for the task of taking the gatehouse, and twelve more to support. Leading them to the palisade walls to right of the gate they crouched, the walls weren't very high and could easily be scaled. Two men pressed their backs against the wall side by side while a third placed both feet in their cupped hands, slowly they lifted him up to look. He scanned the wall then gave the signal for more archers to follow. Ten more archers leaned against the wall and raised another five archers up, when all were level, the first gave a hand signal, pulling themselves up and over the wall the archers lay flat on the walkway.

Beside the brasier two Dornach warriors hunched forward to warm their hands against the cold. The first archer signalled for another to join him and indicated a target, both notched, drew and loosed their arrows simultaneously, notching arrows again they paused. Both arrows thumped into their targets, and both with a clear head shot, one fell back off his stool while the other slumped against the palisade wall. The archers, staying low, slowly crept forwards, on reaching the dead guards they removed the arrows and repositioned the guards as best they could. The square open platform where the brasier stood lay splattered with scarlet, trickling down to a square hatch.

A ladder poked through the mouth of the hatch, leading to a pit of darkness below. The lead archer signalled the others to join him, stepping carefully down the ladder and into the gatehouse, the second archer followed on as the remainder crouched low by the brasier. Inside it was dark and cold, the dim light from a lantern hanging on the wall cast a pale glow around the narrow rectangular room. A weapon rack lined one wall, bows, spears and swords resting against it. In the corner stood a large oak storage cabinet, a table and two chairs opposite. A small door led outside and into the yard, the first archer gently pulled on the rope doorhandle, opening it slowly. The yard was empty, in the distance he could make out silhouettes of various huts and sheds, but no light or movement. Signalling for the second archer to follow, the pair of them cautiously entered the yard. Keeping low, moving along the side of the gate house and around to the gate. Two thick wooden beams stretched across the gate securing it firmly against its frame. The archers took a side each, gently lifting one of the beams off its iron hooks, then carefully placing it to one side. They repeated the process for the next beam and the gate became loose, like the bursting of a dam the archers waiting outside slipped through the half open gate and filled the shadows of the gate house.

Upon seeing this, Conrach shuddered clenching his hands, frantically he gestured for the remaining troops to advance. Conrach joined them as they moved cautiously towards the gatehouse, slowly walking their horses to avoid arousing attention. Inside, the first troop of archers swiftly crossed the open yard to a single wooden guard room. The amber radiance of an oil lamp cast its warming glow through cracks in the door, complimenting a delicate crackle of a log fire beyond. Four archers carefully notched arrows and drew back on their bows as a fifth took hold of the door latch. Squeezing a thumb on the latch, it clicked and he swung open the door. Rushing in, four archers loosed arrows into four resting guards, they notched again as three more archers entered behind them, daggers drawn. The floor turned a crimson red as life twitched out of the dying. The room was warm and cosy, unfitting the violence which had just occurred. Quietly they moved through the building, checking each room for occupants. 'Four guards are not enough for this place.' muttered Burwell as he examined the interior of the guard house. 'There must be a patrol out somewhere in this compound, we need to find them before Conrach arrives with the horses. Quickly, search the area, kill all you find!'

The archers left the building and started to disperse in units of four, staying low and moving fast, one unit went back to the gate house, climbing the palisade wall then crouching low, they began to move clockwise along the top of the wall. Burwell ran back to the gatehouse to halt the main body of troops from entering. As they approached, he ordered more archers inside to start clearing the remaining buildings, Conrach joined him.

'What's the hold up, we need to move fast!'

'We haven't found all the guards, there must be a patrol out.'

'Well hurry up, we need to get back as soon as possible, burn the place down if you have to!'

Burwell acknowledged as more archers filtered through and into the yard. He then ordered the horses into line along the wall and out of sight. Joining a group of six archers entering the gate, Burwell led them towards the storage warehouses. To the left, archers were now filing through the large wooden door to the cookhouse, where earlier that day Ackron's warriors had fed. The mess hall filled with a comforting, homely smell of cooking about it, benches and tables all laid out ready for the next meal, a meal now unlikely to be served. Outside it was dark, crisp-cold and silent, as the archers began spreading out around the complex. Burwell led his archers towards the first warehouse door, it was barred, they moved around the side of the building when something in the distance caught Burwell's eye, a moving shadow silhouetted by an amber light against the wall.

'Guards!' Burwell whispered, his archers, sinking low on one knee, waited. Three shadows slowly came into view, approaching along the side of the building, unaware. Six archers notched their arrows, slowly taking up tension on their bow strings. The first of the guards turned the corner followed by two more carrying oil lamps.

'Loose!' called Burwell, six arrows lanced out into the darkness towards the bewildered patrol. The first guard fell back instantly as two arrows struck home, hard into his head and throat. Four more arrows needled through the darkness and into the remaining guards, thumping them backwards against the wall of the warehouse, as the last guard was hit, his lamp smashed to the ground. Oil splashed across the floor bursting into flame and instantly igniting the guard's clothing, screaming and thrashing as three more arrows silenced his pain, the damage had been done. Flaming oil spread causing the other lamp to explode into flames, and as Burwell watched, the sound of a bell began to franticly toll in the distance. 'Put out the flames! Quickly!' Burwell rushed forward as the burning oil now spread along and up the walls of the warehouse, fingers of flame lapping and caressing the greasy timbers, reaching up to the roof.

'Break open the doors we need to empty this fast!'

The archers began hacking at the lock and levering open the doors, by now Conrach could see and hear the chaos unfold, he ordered the horses inside and towards the warehouse. The Yarromite archers were now starting to engage in fighting as every member of the camp was panicked into action.

Sergeant Morraine burst out of his quarters brandishing a poleaxe in one hand and a short sword in the other. Two archers turned in shock as they ran past him, Morraine thrust hard with the axe into the chest of the farthest and slashed a cross-cut through the throat of the closest with his sword. Without so much as a breath his axe swung again, lightning fast, shattering a half-drawn bow and crashing into the jawbone of its holder. An arrow struck deep into his leg and then another into his side, he swung again knocking a dagger from the hand of one archer then thumping hard into the chest of another. Morraine was ferocious, his eyes bright with rage as his poleaxe swung and spilled the blood of Yarromovia. The scarlet flames from the burning warehouse lit up the alleyway while smoke swirled in a fiery cloud. Morraine was joined by three more Dornach warriors. Slashing, kicking and punching they fought hard for their lives, and for Dornachrov, yet they were heavily outnumbered. The archers drew back out of striking distance, and as they did, they cleared the way for arrows to fill. The Yarromite archers loosed at will, Morraine was struck again in the chest, he staggered forward as another arrow lanced through the side of his neck. The cold air filled with a warm blood-red mist as Morraine fell, a swarm of arrows found their mark, and Morraine's warriors fell beside their leader.

The ringing of the bell was silenced, as Conrach hurried the horses into the burning warehouse.

'Quickly fill the saddlebags, take all you can!'

Lancers ripped open crates packing the contents into saddlebags. Loading horses as fast as they were led into the building. Conrach, dithered around in fear and excitement, barking instructions at everyone in sight. The fire was now out of control as Burwell and the archers continued to break down the doors of the other warehouses. As soon as one building was opened the horses entered and the packing began. It was dark and confusing, but the flames offered enough light, enabling the invaders in their plundering.

Thick plumes of smoke billowed high into the clear night sky, illuminated orange by the burning timbers below. Horses were held tight on reins, led in, packed, and led out again to be lined up outside of the gatehouse. When every horse and every saddlebag was filled, Conrach ordered the archers to pack what they could into their shoulder bags and rejoin the horse troop.

The scene was carnage, not a single Dornach warrior or miner who could be found was spared, corpses lay strewn like leaves in the autumn fall. Fires catching the roofs of adjacent buildings and edging their fiery grasp slowly downwards towards what remained of the last stocks of ember pearl. While the fires did their work, the cavalry of Yarromovia cantered out through the open gates of the palisade and into the blackness of the night.

Chapter 19
Gathering the Pieces

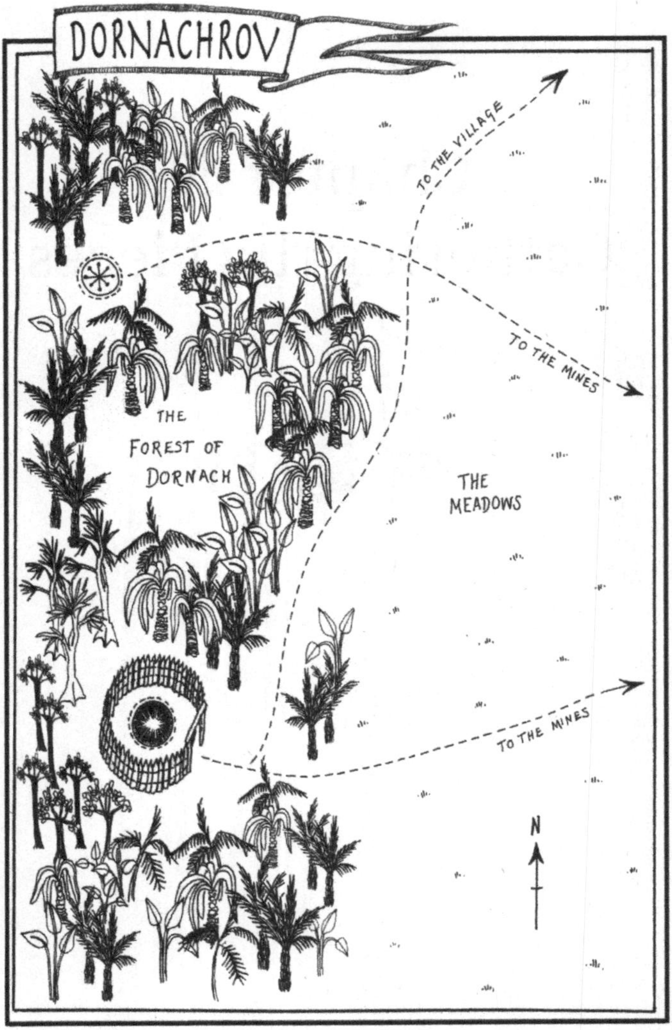
DORNACHROV
TO THE VILLAGE
TO THE MINES
THE FOREST OF DORNACH
THE MEADOWS
TO THE MINES
N

Shelaine paused in her tracks, raising a hand and pointing ahead 'We're too late!' In the distance, the sky flickered orange, fireflie sparks climbing into the smoke-filled air. The warriors stopped and looked up from the darkness of the track. Like the early hue of a sunrise, the horizon glowed pale in the heat of flames, they stood frozen for a moment.

'Keep moving! We have to reach the mines!' Shouted Ackron, the warriors marched on at a faster, desperate pace. Reaching the crest of a hill, the full picture began to take shape; they could just make out the dancing flame tips swirling and rising through the air. Sparks disappearing skyward into blackness. Then, without warning, the sky ahead of them flashed into shards of gold and orange, erupting outward with volcanic brilliance. Within seconds, the sonic wave reached them, shaking the ground where they stood. The thunderous roar continued and dragged out in slow motion as the view ahead of them turned black.

'Keep moving! Keep moving!' Ackron screamed although it resembled a muffled whisper to the rest, grabbing and pushing the warriors forward he began to run. Doon was ahead of him with Shelaine, followed by Tom and Damien.

Ronat stood in the entrance of the Elder's hut, the sky black dark above him, with a hint of moonlight offering a silvered frosting to the dwellings beneath. There had been no word from Thon *they should be here now*. In the distance, he could see the first hint of dawn creeping up above the hills. He paused for a moment, it didn't look right, it was a clear night, but dawn seemed a little earlier than usual. Raising a hand to his brow he blocked any peripheral light to try and get a better view. This wasn't dawn, it was too concentrated, it should be cast across the whole sky, preceded by an icy greyness. Ronat called to his Sergeant.

'What do you make of that?' Pointing across the valley.

The sergeant squinted 'Looks like a fire over the hill Sir.'

'In the direction of the mines, awaken the guard, this can only mean one thing, invasion!' Replied Ronat.

'Yes Sir!'

Within moments the sound of a horn blew deep and long across the town, followed by the sound of dogs barking.

'Guards! Stand to arms! Stand to arms!'

The reserve guard of Dornachrov began to stumble from their homes, half-dressed they smartened themselves as they formed up on the square.

It was not Ronat's wish to deploy these troops, as they were the last resort, destined for the defence of the town, but he had no choice. Two hundred Dornach citizens stood before him, groggy from sleep and damp in the cold of the night. These were not warriors, they were not even fighters, they were a mix of farm workers, young men and women who were able to use a bow or swing a sword, Ronat stepped forward.

'People of Dornachrov, our lands have once again become the victim of the brutal and savageness of Yarromovia. Our friends from Thon I'm sure will assist, but I have had no word yet of their arrival. As I address you now, I fear we are out manoeuvred and outnumbered, and so I must ask for your help, your sacrifice in this twilight of our peace. Dornachrov, is besieged and we must pick up arms to break that siege. It is my belief that the Yarromites are raiding our mines right now, and I need your help to prevent this. I cannot, and will not force you to join me in this battle, I accept that we are all peaceful folk here, and so I invite you to march with me now for what might be our last march, a march for Dornachrov!'

Ronat turned to his Sergeant, nodded gratefully for the service he had given, then stepped off down the track towards the meadow. His Sergeant followed on, the crowd behind him murmured, the muffled voices grew louder,

'For Dornachrov.'

'March for Dornachrov, march for Dornachrov!'

'March for Dornachrov!'

The voices of the young and old, of men and women came together and roared as one.

'March for Dornachrov!'

'Shouldn't we be heading to the mines Sir?' Asked his Sergeant.

'I feel the mines may already be lost.' Ronat replied, choking back the emotion from the pride he felt for his followers. 'If the Yarromites did invade, they came for the ember pearl, and we can't afford to let them get away with it. We are heading to the passing place.'

The gatehouse stood scorched with gates wide open, everything around them was blackened and charred from the explosion. Thick, damp smoke hung in the air, clinging to the throat with every breath. Where the warehouses should have been lay a huge smouldering crater, splinters of timber protruding from the ground like skeletons of what once remained. The buildings across the yard were still recognisable, but badly damaged. Doon crossed the yard cautiously; he could make out lifeless bodies on the ground, softer, rounder in shape than the splintered timber. Some were too charred to identify, while others looked like they were sleeping. He crept through the alleyways, carefully looking for survivors. An impossible task he thought, but he felt compelled to. Then he realised his worst fear, the person he did not want to find here, stuck with arrows, charred and lifeless, his uncle Morraine. Doon fell to his knees weeping beside Morrain's lifeless body. Shelaine stood a short distance away, as Tom and Damien approached from behind. Putting out a hand Shelaine stopped them 'Come, give him space.' She whispered, they slowly turned retracing their steps to the yard.

The processing buildings seemed untouched by the explosion, with the exception of a soot-blackened facade, the fire having been extinguished by the force of the blast. Shelaine, Tom and Damien looked inside the first workshop. Dust and smoke wafted and settled as they entered, but other than that, the mine carts and machinery seemed fine. Then, from the far corner of the workshop, a small figure crawled out from behind one of the carts, covered in soot and with a bloodied face, he staggered over. Damien walked forward.

'It's ok, you're safe now.' If the boy heard he didn't acknowledge, just reached an arm over Damien's shoulder and staggered out of the building with him, blood trickling from his ears.

Several mine workers cautiously started to emerge from the mines and followed the cart tracks down to the processing yard. Shocked, they approached and began to cautiously search for more survivors. It was hard to imagine how anyone could have survived this, yet some did. Most of the buildings were built with thick timbers; blast walls had also been constructed to direct any blast upwards, and it was these that helped protect the majority of the accommodation and processing buildings.

A pale grey silvered sky slowly began to illuminate the night's events, as dawn approached. The heat of the charred earth and stench of smouldering timbers filled the lungs and reddened the eyes. Ackron gathered a party of warriors outside, leading them in search of tracks, it wasn't long before they found what they were looking for. Hoof prints, and plenty of them leading off downhill in the direction of Dornachrov and the passing circle. It was no use, the Yarromites were too fast and far ahead of them. Without horses the warriors of Thon and Dornachrov could never catch up, a better defence was required.

Doon instructed his warriors to gather the dead and prepare a burial mound. Slowly, lines of covered corpses began to form along the palisade wall, while sunrise painted tangerine clouds high above them.

Shelaine, Tom and Damien met with Ackron by the gatehouse, they sat beside a fallen tree as Doon approached.

'We can only hope Ronat received our message and made it to the passing circle.' said Ackron, scraping at the scorched earth with his boot.

'Assuming he even managed to gather enough warriors from the outlying villages.' Added Doon as he sat with the rest.

'We could never reach the passing circle in time anyway, and the troops are exhausted.' Replied Ackron.

'Horses, we need horses.' Shelaine interrupted.

'We don't have any, it's rumoured the Yarromites stole or killed all of them in Dornachrov, and Thon is pretty much the same, Hagleen Castle is the only place that has them.' Replied Ackron.

'Then we need help from Cregheligan; we have horses there, and mounted archers. We are a peaceful race, but after the Yarromites deceived us, we decided to take precautions to defend ourselves.'

'We should meet with Ronat and seek the Elder's guidance on this.' Advised Doon.

Ackron nodded 'I agree. Once we are finished helping out here, we should make our way back to the village. We don't know what the Yarromites have planned.'

Ronat led the reserve guard out of Dornachrov and through the fields towards the forest. The sky turned from grey to orange as the night ebbed away. A shiver of cold ran through him as the dampness of dawn crept in. In the distance he could make out the gnarled bark of tree trunks indicating the edge of the forest, while behind him, eager and loyal, marched the rear guard of Dornachrov.

Entering the forest he could smell the horses, a thick and pungent aroma. The track was gnarled, churned by hooves and covered in muck. Ronat quickened the pace, a feint green canopy gradually came to life above them, softly painted by a pale sky beyond. They were close, close enough to smell the grassy breath of the Yarromite cavalry and their leather saddles.

Struggling to hold back his excitement, Conrach boasted to Burwell.

'They were so unprepared; we could have taken the village too and cleansed these lands of their filth. Little better than vermin, they could all be put to better use working for the Emperor.'

Burwell nodded 'One mission at a time ensures a greater

chance of success.'

'None of this is a matter of chance Burwell, this is down to superiority! The Yarromites are of pure blood, not the sewage that runs through the veins of this scum. We will return and they will know their place in our realm, to serve their masters.'

The column of horses trotted its way along a heavy mud track to the passing circle. Burwell called in the rearguard as the archers and lancers dismounted. The lancers began to recover their weapons and refit their armour, each helping one another to adjust the leather straps attaching their breastplates. Conrach rode to the front of the column and positioned himself in the passing circle, sliding the book from his pouch, he turned to the page which read "Yarromovia" 'Hurry, we need to get back!'

Burwell acknowledged and began to marshal the half-dressed troops into column.

From the depth of the forest a call rang out, then a flurry of arrows flickered out of the trees, and like a swarm of hornets they stung hard. Horses reared and screams shattered the stillness of dawn, as the citizens of Dornachrov took their revenge. Arrows loosed through trees, less than thirty paces from the confused Yarromite raiders, riderless horses bolted into the forest as lancers fought to control them.

'Head to the circle!' Screeched Conrach as he began to recite the passage. The ground trembled, horses stamped and lurched forward, as the world ahead of them began to fade from view.

'Forward! Forward!' screamed Burwell, lancers and archers ran and galloped towards the portal, some lancers fought to drag their horses. Burwell, still mounted rallied his troops as best he could, but by now the Dornachs had started to close in, fighting hand to hand. Horses, lancers and archers scrambled with all they could carry towards the portal, leaving a trail of horrors behind.

'We have to go now Burwell! We can't afford to lose the book!' Shouted Conrach.

Burwell spurred his horse forward charging into the abyss, behind him a trail of stragglers followed on. Turning his horse Conrach kicked back hard and bolted through. The portal flickered and began to close as the remaining Yarromite warriors ran to join their comrades. The portal began to fade and shimmer; screams echoed through as the last of the Yarromites ran toward it's fading light, as Dornach's warriors closed in.

'Stand still and lay down your arms!' Ordered Ronat, a scattering of Yarromite warriors stood before them, defeated and exhausted. 'Lay down your arms now or die!' Ronat shouted, the Yarromites obayed.

The Dornach guard rounded up the prisoners while others picked through the abandoned belongings of the Yarromite invaders. Breastplates and lances lay scattered among the dead, several wounded Yarromites were gathered together and tended to. Prisoners and those who had less severe wounds were instructed to gather the bodies of those killed and place them beside the treeline, here the Yarromites began burying their dead.

'No casualties taken on our side, the Yarromites lost thirty-two troops and we have twenty-four prisoners Sir.' The Sergeant continued, running through his list of items retrieved, mostly weapons and armour, but also a few horses had been rounded up nearby. Some of those horses still carried packs filled with ember pearl.

'Good work! Arrange for those and the prisoners to be escorted back to the village once the burial has been completed.' Ordered Ronat.

The grave took the form of a single trench, less than

knee deep it stretched off into the forest. When the last shovel of earth was thrown, Ronat arranged for the prisoners' wrists to be bound before being led back to Dornachrov. The rear guard followed on, leaving the passing circle clear, but for a speckling of broken arrows, deeply churned into the muddy clearing.

Midmorning brought the warmth of the day, evaporating the dampness of dawn and coaxing insects back to flight, as the train of prisoners, warriors and horses threaded its way across the meadows.

Once rested, Ackron ordered his warriors back to the portal with what ember pearl they had left. Their job was to continue with the work of bolstering defences under the command of Captain Reeval. Doon and the remainder helped organise the mine area. The miners who remained began to clean up and assess the damage, the processing plant was mostly intact and the mines were untouched, but they would need more workers and guards to protect them. Leaving what few warriors he had left at the mines, Doon, Ackron, Tom, Damien and Shelaine left and began the journey back to the village. The day was warming, and with it, a strange sense of calm could be felt. There was little conversation on the journey back, whether that was because of tiredness, sadness, or both, it was hard to tell. Tom ached beyond belief, exhausted and tortured by blisters he walked on. He was afraid, he hadn't confronted the full force of the Yarromites, but he had seen first-hand what they were capable of on two occasions now, and it frightened him. Damien didn't seem as concerned, but on the inside, he felt it far worse than the retreat from Hagleen Castle.

Ronat was standing in the square when Doon arrived, Doon's eyes welled with tears as they hugged. 'Morraine is dead.' Was all that Doon could manage before sobbing into Ronat's shoulder. The pair of them looked upon Morraine as a mentor, the grandfather of Dornach's warriors.

'We should let the Elder know.' Ronat, putting an arm around his friend, led Doon into the hut while the rest of the group sat beside the square in the shade of a large tree. The tree was filled with tiny songbirds, each lightly twittering and singing in the warmth of the noon sunlight. Herran walked around from the back of the Elder's hut carrying a tray filled with food and drinks for them.

'Herran, thank you! It's good to see you again.'

Damien walked over to help. Tom smiled, there was a time Tom would have mocked his friend, but not now, he felt the pain of the past few days weigh heavy on his mind, *is this what growing up feels like?* he thought.

Ackron took two mugs of sweet tea from the tray and offering one, he turned to Shelaine 'Tell me more about these horses you have in Cregheligan.'

Letter to the reader

If you're reading this then thank you, you've acquired my book and I hope you enjoy it. This is my first novel and it's intended to be the second in a series. Some books from this first edition will be distributed in freely accessible book exchanges, and that might be how you came by it. It would be nice to hear what you thought of it, so feel free to email a review. It's a story that I came up with around twenty years ago, one that I've carried until I had the time to write and publish it. Many of the places are inspired from childhood adventures, as real to me today as they were fifty years ago. The sequel to this is now in the planning stage, and you can find out more by following me on Instagram: karl_r_harter or through my website: www.karlrharter.net

Best wishes,

Karl.

About the author

Karl R. Harter was born and raised in Hindley, Wigan, and now lives in Surrey. Having started his working life in engineering and construction, he later joined the Royal Air Force in 1989 and served for ten years working in air defence. After leaving the RAF he worked in the field of information technology and later retrained to become a therapeutic counsellor. Throughout his life he has enjoyed writing as an escape and adventure. As a young boy he was inspired that someone from the world he grew up in could be a successful writer. That someone, was John Farrimond, an author who lived a few doors up on the same street where Karl was born. The Lost Book of Cregheligan is Karl's first novel, and the first book to be written in this series.